Charlotte looked through her hanging clothes, trying to decide what to wear to eat with the captain.

The schedule clearly stated that the first night was not formal, so she finally decided on a soft floral cotton gauze dress. She liked the way the full skirt swirled around her legs. It made her feel feminine. Why that made any difference tonight, she didn't know.

Before leaving the room, they studied the map to see where the main dining room was. Charlotte folded the map and stuck it in her tiny shoulder bag in case they needed it later. They took the elevator up to deck four. A cruise employee waited to show passengers the way. When they arrived at the dining room, Chelle handed the maitre d' the invitation. He immediately led them toward a table on a raised platform surrounded by railings. Charlotte glanced around, taking in the burgundy plush carpeting as well as the muted draperies on the windows, or were they portholes? But they weren't round. The high-ceilinged room was open in the middle with balcony seating on the deck above. This dining room was like an upscale restaurant on land, except the floor was not completely steady. Charlotte had trouble with the movement of the ship for about an hour, but now she had her sea legs.

When the maitre d' pulled out her chair, she glanced at the other people at the table. Five besides herself and Chelle—a couple who held hands as if they were newlyweds, an older couple, and the captain.

Charlotte couldn't believe her eyes. That man on the deck, the one with the piercing blue eyes, was the captain, and he sat right beside her. Suddenly, the comfortably air-conditioned room felt too warm and something inside her quaked. She worried that she wouldn't be able to eat a thing with her stomach acting that way. Charlotte had been sure she wouldn't have a problem with motion sickness, but now she wondered.

LENA NELSON DOOLEY lives in Texas with her husband James. They are active in several ministries of their church. She speaks at retreats and conferences. Both she and James are interested in missions and have been on several mission trips. A full-time author and editor, Lena holds a BA in Speech and Drama. She has had several novels published by **Heartsong Presents** and two novella collections. Visit her web site at: www.LenaNelsonDooley.com.

Books by Lena Nelson Dooley

HEARTSONG PRESENTS
HP54—Home to Her Heart
HP492—The Other Brother
HP584—His Brother's Castoff
HP604—Double Deception
HP615—Gerda's Lawman
HP656—Pirate's Prize

Never Say Never

Lena Nelson Dooley

Heartsong Presents

Dedicated to the leaders of my Ladies' Life Groups at Gateway Church—Suzette Roach, Aja Schiewe, and Arnita Taylor. Thank you for pouring the love of the Lord into my life and encouraging me to move in my giftings.

And as always, this book is dedicated to James, the man God created just for me, whose strengths meet my weaknesses and who draws strength from me. Our marriage is one of the best things that ever happened to me.

A note from the Author:
I love to hear from my readers! You may correspond with me by writing:

> **Lena Nelson Dooley**
> **Author Relations**
> **PO Box 721**
> **Uhrichsville, OH 44683**

ISBN 1-59789-056-1

NEVER SAY NEVER

All scripture quotations are taken from the King James Version of the Bible.

All of the characters and events in this book are fictitious. Any resemblance to actual persons, living or dead, or to actual events is purely coincidental.

Our mission is to publish and distribute inspirational products offering exceptional value and biblical encouragement to the masses.

PRINTED IN THE U.S.A.

prologue

A light melody invaded Charlotte Halloran's dream. *Oh no, it can't be morning yet.* Her right hand snaked from under the floral sheet that almost covered her head—reaching, searching for the offending clock radio. After finding it, she pushed the SNOOZE button and settled back into comfort. But the sound came again, playing the same tune Philip had programmed as her cell phone ring tone. Charlotte pushed up to sit on the side of the bed. She needed to be fully awake to make any sense of a phone call. As she reached for the phone, she noticed the time—3:09 a.m.—and the other side of the bed remained empty. What was Philip doing out this late?

When he left after supper, he told her that he wanted to finish all the paperwork at the office so they could spend Saturday together. Their teenage daughter, Chelle, would be working at the youth carwash to help pay for summer camp. Charlotte and Philip could have a rare day alone. He said he would be late getting home, but after three o'clock was ridiculous.

Charlotte placed the instrument to her ear. "Philip, where are you?" She didn't care how harsh her voice sounded. She didn't like him staying out this late. Danger roamed the highways this time of night.

Her comment was greeted by a startled gasp then deafening silence. Instinctively, Charlotte knew it wasn't Philip on the other end of the line. Whom had she just spoken to? She hoped it wasn't a criminal or some kind of pervert. She had just informed the caller that her husband wasn't home. "Look, I don't know who you are—" Charlotte's hand shook. She didn't like crank phone calls. Ever since Philip joined the police force, they kept their home phone number unlisted, so they didn't receive them often. "And I don't know how you got our number, but I'm going to hang up, and you can just forget you tried to make this crank call."

"Please, Mrs. Halloran, don't hang up."

The tentative masculine voice sounded familiar. Where had she heard it before? She had a hard time thinking when awakened from such a sound sleep.

Charlotte rubbed her temples with her left hand. "Why not? Do you have any idea what time it is?"

"Yes, I'm aware of the time." The voice sounded firm and gentle. "This is George Mallory."

Why is Philip's boss calling me at this time in the morning?

"Mrs. Halloran. . .Charlotte, there's been an accident."

Charlotte waited for more information, but it wasn't forthcoming. "Philip wasn't on duty tonight. He was at the insurance office." Charlotte didn't like the geyser of panic welling inside her. Philip didn't like to work a second job to make ends meet. Why couldn't the city pay their police officers enough to provide a decent living for a family?

"I know. Listen, I'm right outside in a squad car. I didn't want to just ring the doorbell. Please come to the front door. I'll be waiting on the porch. Okay?"

Charlotte agreed and hung up. She stumbled to the closet and pulled out her fleece robe—the one Philip had given her last Christmas. Her fingers fumbled, and she dropped the blue fabric to the floor before she finally managed to pull it on and belt it around her waist. Then, she ran a brush through her curls to tame them. As she did, she glanced in the mirror. She startled at her terror-filled eyes. When she tried to put the brush back on the dresser, it fell to the carpet.

After picking it up and placing it precisely on the middle of the polished pecan dresser, Charlotte hurried to the front door. She peeked through the peephole to make sure it really was Captain Mallory. She grasped the doorknob but didn't turn it—didn't want to open the door. Something fearful waited for her on the other side. She heard a tentative knock and, finally, opened the door.

Phyllis Johnson, Philip's partner, accompanied Captain Mallory. The grim expressions on their faces did nothing to calm Charlotte's fears.

"Please come in." She led the way into the den. "Would you like to sit down?"

"Maybe you should, Charlotte." Phyllis perched on the edge of the turquoise sofa, and Charlotte dropped into the cushions on the other end.

Charlotte had always liked Philip's partner. They often teased about them being twins because of their names. Charlotte knew Philip trusted Phyllis with his life, and Charlotte had, too.

"What's this all about?" she couldn't keep from asking. But in her heart, she knew. Something had happened to Philip. Something pretty bad, judging by the way his coworkers were acting.

"There's no easy way to say this, Mrs. Halloran." Captain Mallory sounded so formal. He usually joked and laughed a lot. Maybe that was why she hadn't recognized his voice on the phone. "On his way home, Philip had stopped to help a stranded motorist up on Airport Freeway. You know Philip never could pass by anyone in need of help."

Charlotte nodded. Philip always said, "What if it were

you? I'd want someone to stop and help. Wouldn't you?"

"He pulled over after passing the other car. The man in the car came up and talked to Philip. When they were walking back to the second vehicle, a driver drifted off the road. Philip pushed the motorist out of the way and took the brunt of the hit from an SUV."

Charlotte had never felt faint in her life—until now. She lowered her head and took a deep breath. Just how badly had Philip been hurt? And why were they sitting here? They should all be on their way to the hospital.

"You know the bars close at two on Saturday mornings." Phyllis didn't like drunk drivers any better than Philip did, and now one of them had harmed Charlotte's husband. "We think the driver had spent most of the evening drinking. At least it wasn't a hit and run. We have him under arrest."

With her heart sinking, Charlotte raised her head to look at Phyllis. "What hospital did they take him to? H. E. B.?" Then it hit her like a second impact of that SUV. The captain referred to Philip using the past tense. A ball of fear settled inside her, not leaving her much space to breathe.

Phyllis glanced at Captain Mallory, whose grim expression looked anything but comfortable. "They didn't take him to a hospital, Mrs. Halloran." He raked in a deep breath. "We had to call the coroner."

Dead? Philip is dead? No, he can't be. Charlotte leaned over and clutched her stomach, trying to stop the deep, agonizing pain that knifed through her. At that moment, something vital—the womanly intimate part of her that she and Philip had shared—died, too. Life as she had known it ended for all time.

one

Bright Louisiana sunshine painted everything golden as Charlotte and Chelle Halloran stepped from the airplane into the New Orleans airport. High humidity made the day seem more like summer than springtime. An employee of the travel agency met them. The young man helped to collect their luggage and load it into the cruise shuttle van. Chelle sat by the window so she could see everything on the long ride into New Orleans.

Charlotte couldn't understand why a city would have its airport so far from town. The travel agent had to book their flight before noon so they would have plenty of time to get to the cruise dock on the Mississippi River. The ship sailed from New Orleans down the river to the Gulf of Mexico later today, then on to the Caribbean.

"What are those?" Chelle pointed toward a cemetery.

"I really don't know," Charlotte answered as she studied what looked like small concrete vaults on top of the ground, in regimented rows across the parklike setting. Some of the cemeteries in the Dallas-Fort Worth area had mausoleums, but they didn't look like these structures.

"Everyone in New Orleans is buried above the ground." The van driver answered Chelle's question without taking his eyes from the freeway. "New Orleans is so low, and the water table so high, they can't be buried in the ground. The bodies would float right out of their graves at the first sign of rain." Then he laughed at his own joke, his chocolate face wreathed in a smile.

9

His strong Cajun accent sounded rich as molasses, making it hard for Charlotte to understand. She really had to listen closely to catch everything.

What a strange way to bury people. Charlotte decided this wasn't a subject she really wanted to dwell on right now. They were taking the cruise to get away from memories on the first anniversary of Philip's death, and here she was looking at cemeteries in New Orleans. She searched for different types of architecture and hoped it wouldn't take too much longer to reach the cruise dock. The typical homes in Bedford, Texas, where she lived, were definitely different from those that lined the freeway in the suburbs of New Orleans. As they got closer to downtown, they drove through industrial and shopping districts before they passed the Super Dome. Philip had planned to come to New Orleans the next time the Super Bowl was played there. He had always wanted to see the famed stadium. Even though the city suffered extreme damage during past storms, like the proverbial phoenix, it had risen again to the vital city that spread before Charlotte's eyes.

When they arrived at the dock area, the van driver unloaded their luggage and carried it into the building where Voyageana Cruise Line accepted passengers. They wouldn't allow passengers to board the ship until 2:00 p.m., but they did attach luggage tags with cabin numbers to the bag handles and set them aside to load on the boat. Piles of luggage formed two lines down the length of the building. Charlotte hoped her and Chelle's bags wouldn't get mixed up with someone else's. She didn't even want to think about facing eight days and seven nights without her essentials.

"Mom, I'm hungry." Chelle was always hungry, but it had been a long time since breakfast.

Charlotte asked the cruise line representative where they

could get something to eat. After being directed to the River Walk, they found a little bistro. Along the way, Charlotte and her teenage daughter tasted some of the samples of spicy Cajun dishes that were offered by other establishments. After they were seated at a wrought iron table, Charlotte was glad the bistro also served sandwiches—without the hot seasoning.

While they ate, Charlotte hoped she hadn't made a mistake taking this trip. Philip had planned on the family going on a cruise when Chelle graduated from high school. That was still a year off, but Charlotte decided to move the plans up, hoping it would help both of them. She was running from the memory of that fateful night last year when she lost her husband. By taking Chelle on this cruise, she hoped to erase some of the horrible memories, if that was possible.

After eating lunch, when they arrived back at the cruise dock building, they were told they could board. They waited in line to receive their room key cards, but the line moved quickly.

"Chelle, you know how important it is for you to keep up with the key card, don't you?" Charlotte almost hesitated to hand it over.

"Ma'am." The young man in a cruise line uniform came around from behind the desk. "How would you like to have one of these?" He held out a lanyard with the name of the ship on it. "This way, she can wear it around her neck."

Chelle got that stubborn look that said, *How dorky*, but Charlotte didn't give her a chance to voice her protest. "We'll take two, if that's all right."

"Sure. Just let me punch a hole in the key cards."

It must have been a good idea, because Charlotte heard the people behind them asking for lanyards, too.

She and Chelle stepped out into the warm Louisiana

sunshine. The white ship rocked gently in the water. A lengthy stretch of dock spanned the distance between where the two of them stood and the moored ship. The glistening vessel looked huge, as tall as a seven- or eight-story building, at least above the waterline. Charlotte wondered how deep the boat went below the surface. Sunlight glinted off brass railings on three upper decks, and bright flags, strung on lines that stretched from the front to the back of the ship, fluttered in the wind. The *Pearl of the Ocean*. Voyageana Cruise Line's newest ship. According to the brochure, this was only the second voyage. Gleaming in the sunlight, it did look like a pearl. Very inviting.

The back half of the dock was completely shaded from the sunlight. A photographer had set up there making each group of passengers stop in front of a large canvas containing a picture of the ship. He took pre-boarding portraits before they continued toward the small shuttle bus.

After she and Chelle climbed up the three steps, they took the last two seats, right behind the driver. The short drive only took a couple of minutes.

"I don't know why we couldn't have walked to the ship." Chelle sounded peeved.

Charlotte hoped she wasn't going to gripe about everything that happened. "Just relax and enjoy the nice things they're doing for us."

At the ship, another line of passengers led across the boarding ramp that bridged the dock to the hatch of the ship. Evidently they had a security checkpoint just inside. She and Chelle took their places at the end of the line. There was no turning back now. Charlotte took a deep breath and followed her daughter, moving a few steps closer.

Charlotte glanced up at the ship, which looked enormous.

Rows of portholes lined the level they would be entering. On the deck above, larger windows stretched across the length. Even farther up, the rooms had balconies. After counting the rows, Charlotte shook her head. *Why do I always count things?* A long-term, crazy habit that would be hard to break.

She noticed a blond man standing at the rail of one the decks above the entrance to the ship. He stood out in sharp contrast to the blue sky behind him, where a few cottony clouds drifted by.

The man was very tall with broad shoulders and a trim waist. He looked to be at least forty. Probably some kind of officer with all that gold braid on his snow-white uniform. Charlotte's gaze was drawn to his piercing blue eyes, which looked straight at her. For a frozen moment, she felt as if they were the only two people in the world. Something in him connected with something deep inside of her. And it scared her. She was glad she wouldn't have any contact with the officer, whoever he was. She didn't need the kind of complication that feeling could bring. After all, that part of her had died a year ago. She knew she would never experience romantic love again.

ও

Gareth Van den Hout usually didn't watch the passengers come aboard his ship. He would begin meeting them soon enough. So many sought out the captain whenever they could. Today, for some reason, he felt more restless than he had in a long time. So he stepped onto the balcony outside the bridge. With practiced detachment, Gareth watched the passengers in the line, waiting to get inside. As with every trip, there were all kinds of people dressed in myriad ways, some extremely outlandish. Why did they think they needed to dress so differently to go on a cruise? Sometimes he had a hard time not laughing at some of the attire.

His attention quickly settled on two attractive women with curly hair so black that blue light glinted from it—one young, one a little older. While he watched them, the older one looked straight into his eyes. The bright eyes that stared back at him were a wonderful contrast to all that dark hair blowing in the wind. When their gaze connected, a jolt shook him, causing him to want to get to know her better. He had to know where that jolt came from.

Quickly, Gareth turned and walked to the office of his apartment on the deck right below the bridge. He picked up the phone and punched in his purser's cell number.

"Yes, Captain. What can I do for you?"

Gareth didn't know if he would ever get used to all these electronic gadgets. It still startled him when someone knew who he was before he identified himself.

"Doug, I just noticed two women in line to come aboard." Gareth wondered if he was crazy to do this. It was a real departure from his usual behavior on a voyage. "They looked as if they might be mother and daughter. The younger one is tall with long dark hair. The older one looks like her, but is petite and her hair is shorter."

"I see them on the screen," Doug Baxter answered. "They are going through security right now."

"Find out who they are and send them an invitation to dine at the captain's table in the later seating at dinner tonight." Gareth hung up before he had a chance to hear Doug's affirmative answer—or the questions he knew his friend would ask.

❧

After Charlotte and Chelle moved into the ship, a crew-member directed them to the elevators. "Go up to deck five.

You can get information on what's happening today, and they will tell you how soon you may go to your staterooms."

When they stepped off the elevator, another cruise employee pointed them toward the side of what looked like a balcony around the center of the ship. Charlotte moved to the railing and looked up at similar balconies on four more decks. A man who introduced himself as the purser gave out folders of information as he explained what would happen on board. Then they were urged to go to their staterooms. A member of the crew showed them on their map just how to get to their cabin.

Charlotte had saved money on the cruise by booking rooms on one of the lower decks. She and Chelle were directed down a hall toward a different elevator. When the elevator reached deck three, they got off in a sort of lobby.

"Mom, look at these mirrors." Chelle pointed to several slabs of the shiny glass on the wall near the elevators and beside the open stairway. The mirrored tiles were attached in a pattern.

Charlotte studied them a minute before she realized what they were. "It's a world map. Each of the mirrors is one of the continents."

Chelle stopped and cocked her head to look at them again. "You're right, Mom. That's pretty cool."

They read the signs on the corridors that ran down each side of the ship to find which would lead to their cabin. Soon they reached their door, and both of them tried their key cards to make sure they worked. Chelle took a couple of times to get the hang of how to do it just right.

Charlotte was glad to see all their luggage had reached their room. First, she and Chelle checked out their cabin. To the right of the door, a nice-sized closet would hold their hanging clothes and keep their luggage out of the way.

"Mom, look at this tiny bathroom." Chelle had opened the door opposite the closet.

Charlotte glanced in. "It's not so small. We probably could both be in here at the same time, if we need to be."

"Yeah, especially if one of us is in the shower." Chelle pulled the curtain across the opening. "I like the way it curves. And look at the showerhead. It's on a wand."

"Good. In most places, the shower nozzle is too high for me. I can take that one down and use it as a hand shower." Charlotte stepped back into the cabin.

Chelle followed her. "Look, Mom. We even have a couch and a TV. I wonder if they have satellite. Wouldn't that be the only way we could have programming at sea?"

"Probably." Charlotte turned on the switch below the mirrored cabinet above the desk, which faced opposite the couch. Lights surrounded the mirror. "Well, one of us can use this while the other one puts on her makeup and does her hair in the bathroom. That's nice."

Chelle flopped down on one of the beds that lined the walls on either side of a large picture window. Muted aqua-colored drapes framed the glass. "Want me to read this to you?"

"Sure," Charlotte answered as she started unpacking their clothes. She put their underwear and pajamas in the large drawers and hung their other clothes in the closet. There was plenty of room for their toiletries in the corner cabinets beside the desk's lighted mirror.

"Do we want early seating or later seating in the dining room?" Chelle held a pen poised to mark the card they were supposed to turn in with their choices marked on it.

"What times are we talking about?" Charlotte shook out her royal blue after-five dress, wondering why she brought it.

She knew there were a couple of formal nights on a cruise, but she wasn't sure whether or not she was going to participate in any of them.

"Well, early seating is at 6:00 p.m., and late seating is at 8:00 p.m." Chelle rolled over on her stomach and looked up at her mother.

"I'd probably get too hungry if we wait until eight, wouldn't you?" Charlotte dropped onto the other bed and slipped off her sandals.

"Yeah, let's sign up for the early one. But that means breakfast is early, too."

Charlotte picked up some of the information from her folder. "Doesn't it say something about being able to eat breakfast somewhere else besides the dining room?"

"Sure." Chelle looked back at the schedule. "There's an Oceanic Grille on deck nine that serves meals most all day."

"Then breakfast shouldn't be a problem." Charlotte stood up and stretched. A knock sounded on their door. She opened it and peeked out. A crewmember in a white uniform stood outside, so she opened the door wider.

"Madame, I'm Rigoberto, your cabin steward." He held a large white envelope. "I'm here to take care of your every desire. If you need me, I will always be on this section of your deck."

"Thank you, Rigoberto." Charlotte smiled, wondering if she should tip him now. She knew her travel fares included some tip charges with the price of the cruise, but she wasn't sure what all was included in that amount. The purser had said to read all the information before doing anything else. As soon as the steward was gone, she intended to do that. She didn't want to start out with a faux pas.

"Oh, yes, and Madame, I was told by the purser to give this

to you." He extended the envelope.

"Now who can this be from?" Charlotte asked Chelle as she closed the door after thanking the steward.

"Open it and see." Chelle was still as curious as she had been at three years old.

Charlotte turned the envelope over to see if there was any indication as to who sent it; the only thing written on the outside was their names. However, it did bear a gold *Pearl of the Ocean* seal. She loosened the flap, pulled out a card, and read aloud, "The honor of your presence is requested at the captain's table at eight o'clock tonight."

"What?" Chelle shouted. She grabbed the envelope from her mom and turned it over. "It's addressed to both of us. Wow! We're going to eat with the captain on the first night of the cruise. Wow! I guess that rules out the early seating."

❧

Charlotte looked through her hanging clothes, trying to decide what to wear to eat with the captain. The schedule clearly stated that the first night was not formal, so she finally decided on a soft floral cotton gauze dress. She liked the way the full skirt swirled around her legs. It made her feel feminine. Why that made any difference tonight, she didn't know.

Before leaving the room, they studied the map to see where the main dining room was located. Charlotte folded the map and stuck it in her tiny shoulder bag in case they needed it later. They took the elevator up to deck four. A cruise employee waited to show passengers the way. When they arrived at the dining room, Chelle handed the maitre d' the invitation. He immediately led them toward a table on a raised platform surrounded by railings. Charlotte glanced around, taking in the burgundy plush carpeting as well as the muted draperies on the windows. Or were they portholes? But they weren't round. The high-ceilinged room was open in the middle with balcony seating on the deck above. This dining room was like an upscale restaurant on land, except that the floor was not completely steady. Charlotte had trouble with the movement of the ship for about an hour, but now she'd found her sea legs.

When the maitre d' pulled out her chair, she glanced at the other people at the table. Five besides herself and Chelle—a couple who held hands as if they were newlyweds, an older couple, and the captain.

Charlotte couldn't believe her eyes. That man on the deck, the one with the piercing blue eyes, was the captain, and he sat right beside her. Suddenly, the comfortably air-conditioned room felt too warm and something inside her quaked. She worried that she wouldn't be able to eat a thing with her stomach acting this way. Charlotte had been sure she wouldn't have a problem with motion sickness, but now she wondered.

❧

Gareth hoped that what he felt earlier in the afternoon had been a one-time thing, but when the two Halloran women swept into the room, he knew it wasn't. Charlotte. Doug said the woman's name was Charlotte. Her hair was pulled back on the sides and held by combs with pearls, which gleamed among those shiny ebony curls. A becoming blush stained her cheeks with just the right amount of color to set off her blue eyes accented by long lashes. Filmy fabric covered with light-colored flowers floated around her like a cloud as she walked across the room, inspecting everything in it along the way. Then she sank into the chair beside him, and he felt her presence as if she were touching him, but she wasn't. What in the world was wrong with him?

"Mrs. Halloran, welcome to my table." Why did it sound so intimate when he welcomed her, and it hadn't when he welcomed the other two couples? "Is this young woman your sister?" Why had he asked such an inane question? He knew she was her daughter. An idiot could have thought of something better to say.

"My name is Chelle." The girl giggled. She was even younger than he had guessed.

The blush in her mother's cheeks darkened.

"Other people have asked us that before, Captain," Chelle answered. "Mother has always looked young for her age."

a.

Charlotte had heard that often, but this time it made her sound so ancient. She glanced at the captain. He looked intently at her, just as he had earlier in the day.

"And is Mr. Halloran on the cruise with you?" A feminine voice interrupted Charlotte's thoughts.

For a moment, she wondered who asked the question. The older woman on her right was smiling at her.

She gulped back the sob that threatened. "I'm a widow."

"Oh, dearie, I'm so sorry." The woman patted Charlotte's arm. "Don't mind me. My husband is always telling me I'm too inquisitive." She smiled up at the man seated on her other side. "We're the Watsons. And these young folks are our newlyweds, the Nelsons."

Lively conversation buzzed around the table all through the meal as the diverse people got acquainted. Charlotte had a hard time keeping up with it all. She was too aware of the man sitting next to her. She felt every move he made, even though they were several inches apart. Thankfully she wasn't across the table from him. To look into those arresting eyes all evening would have been impossible. Although she had been hungry as they approached the dining room, her appetite deserted her. So she pushed her food around her plate, eating only a few bites. There had been five or six courses, but after she and Chelle returned to their room, Charlotte couldn't remember one thing they were served. This was not supposed to happen to her. If she didn't know better, she would have thought she was experiencing attraction to a person of the opposite sex.

⌖

On other trips, Gareth participated in mild, harmless flirtations with women at his table. And he had thought that was what would happen when he invited the Hallorans tonight. But it wasn't. How could he mildly flirt with the woman when something in her called out to his heart? And why did it? He vowed when Britte died three years ago that he would never go through the pain again. He didn't want a relationship that called for a commitment. But he couldn't imagine any other kind with Charlotte Halloran. And not having a relationship with her was no longer a viable option for him. While he hated to think of her suffering from the grief of a deceased spouse, it had been a relief to find out that she was unattached. Feeling such a strong attraction to a married woman would have been disastrous, and he would never have explored that connection.

Gareth paced across the large expanse of his luxurious apartment. He glanced out into the dark night, watching the lights on the bank of the Mississippi slowly drift by. While they moved down toward the mouth of the great river, the ship couldn't go very fast. Even though this vessel had very little wake, he didn't want to chance swamping small fishing boats that shared the waterway with them. The restlessness that ate at his insides made him want to shift the ship into high gear and sail past these shores at a fast clip. Anything to get away from his disturbing thoughts.

What was he going to do about Charlotte? Of course, he could see that he never came in contact with her again on the voyage. Perhaps that would be best. This crazy night was just a fluke, a blip on the radar of his life. He would forget it happened. . .and forget Charlotte Halloran. . .with her creamy skin, bright blue eyes, and dancing black curls.

He continued to pace from his office, through the living room, to the kitchen, and back, unable to relax until after midnight, when they were free from the mouth of the river. The engines shifted, and the ship sped up for its voyage across the Gulf of Mexico. Now he could go to bed. As he undressed, he reiterated his decision to forget what happened earlier in the day. Then he fell into his king-sized bed to be lulled to sleep by the motion of the gentle waves.

But not this time. When Gareth finally rose, after tossing and turning all night, he realized that he had only slept intermittently. How in the world was he supposed to run a tight ship on so little sleep? Something would have to be done about it. His closest friends on the crew were his first mate, Homer Wilson, and his purser, Doug Baxter. Maybe they should have breakfast together. The two men could speak words of sanity to him, help him move away from this explosive situation.

two

Charlotte left the dining room without lingering to talk to the other passengers. She couldn't even remember what she gave as an excuse. First she tried hiding in her cabin, but although it seemed roomy when they first boarded, she felt like a caged tiger as she paced the small area. When Chelle finally came in from dinner, Charlotte asked if she'd accompany her out on deck for a while so they could get some exercise. She hoped it would calm her nerves enough to sleep. They decided to change into sports clothes for the trek. Charlotte stuffed the map brochure into the pocket of her hooded sweater. Although it was after ten thirty, a lot of people remained on deck, probably excited about the start of the cruise. But that wasn't what kept Charlotte so agitated. The breathless sensation that gripped her chest when the captain looked at her was way too unsettling.

"Why are we going so slow?" Chelle's question caused Charlotte to turn from the rail and look at her daughter, who stood beside one of the young crewmen. Chelle gazed up into his face. "It doesn't feel as if the ship is even moving."

The blond young man smiled at Chelle. "We're still cruising down the Mississippi. If we go any faster, we might disturb small fishing boats sharing the water with us."

"Wow!" Chelle beamed at the attention from the handsome crewman. "I never thought of that."

Charlotte took her daughter's arm. "Let's walk on one of the upper decks."

When they stepped off the elevator on deck ten, only a few people shared the vast space. She pulled the map out of her pocket. According to the brochure, this deck could be used as a jogging track. People probably jogged in the morning or early evening, not at this time of night. But Charlotte liked the isolation. She leaned against the railing and gazed toward where she supposed the bank of the river to be. In the inky blackness, she really couldn't tell. The sky must be overcast, because she didn't see the moon or any stars.

A cluster of lights that might be a house looked far enough away to be on the riverbank. About halfway between those lights and the ship, a single lantern bobbed above the water on one of those fishing boats the crewman mentioned.

"Mom,"—Chelle put her arm around Charlotte—"this is going to be fun. Please don't be so sad about Daddy."

"Okay, honey." Charlotte pulled her daughter close. Chelle probably thought she was still bothered because the woman at dinner had brought up old memories. And she wasn't going to tell her anything different. How could she explain what she didn't understand herself?

Arm in arm, she and Chelle started to walk around the ship.

"Look, Mom." Chelle pointed to the space at the very back. "It's a rock-climbing wall. I want to try that."

Charlotte's gaze traveled up the length of the structure. It jutted out at the top and had various colors and shapes of rocks embedded in the concrete surface. "It doesn't look that safe to me."

"M-o-m." That teenage whine always set Charlotte's teeth on edge. "You know they wouldn't let anything happen to me."

Charlotte didn't like the spark of adventure in her daughter's eyes. She had seen that same glint often enough in her husband's eyes. She knew his tenacity ran through Chelle, too. Maybe Charlotte could interest her in something tamer and safer, and she would forget about trying to climb that thing. If Philip had been with them, he would have encouraged Chelle to do it, but since Charlotte was the only parent, she felt a strong need to protect her only child.

After midnight, the ship entered the Gulf of Mexico and picked up speed. Thinking the walk around the deck and the night sea air would help her sleep, Charlotte suggested they return to their cabin. As they got ready for bed, she hoped the gentle motion of the ship would rock her to sleep. But it didn't. Every time she closed her eyes, Captain Van den Hout's face swam behind the lids. This could not be happening. She would just have to stay out of his way. Surely that wouldn't be difficult on a ship as large as this one. She had experienced a wonderful romance in her past. She knew that other women who had good marriages and lost their husbands wanted to experience it again, but she just couldn't be like them. Why would she want to complicate the future?

When Charlotte awoke, Chelle was not in the stateroom. That wasn't a problem. Chelle was seventeen and about to finish her junior year in high school. She had always been pretty responsible. Besides, she had to be somewhere on the ship. Charlotte figured that if Chelle had finished breakfast, she was out by the pool.

After getting dressed, Charlotte decided to have her meal at the Oceanic Grille instead of in the dining room. Maybe she wouldn't run into the captain there. As she entered the sunlit room with walls of glass, most tables were empty. The only crewmembers present served behind the large buffet lines.

Charlotte filled her plate with more food than she could possibly eat, but her stomach growled with hunger after that fiasco last night. Besides, with so much to choose from—scrambled eggs, a breakfast casserole, French toast, pancakes, waffles, bacon, ham, sausage, various fruits, and biscuits—her plate was full, even though she only took a little bit of several things. At the middle of the room, another buffet setup included cooked cereal, dry cereal, several kinds of sweet rolls and pastries, and bagels. Extra weight really showed on her short figure, but she would have a hard time not gaining any on this trip. Charlotte sat at a table by the windows that looked out over the bow of the ship and started to read a book as she ate her breakfast. Occasionally, she glanced up to take in the expanse of gentle, gray blue waves. The peaceful sight calmed her, and the story moved toward a mystery that pulled her along.

"Charlotte?"

A familiar masculine voice poured over her just like the warm syrup had covered her waffle a few minutes ago. She turned toward the tall officer.

"It is all right for me to call you Charlotte, isn't it?"

All she could do was nod as his intense gaze captured hers.

"And you must call me Gareth." He pulled out the chair across from Charlotte. "May I join you while I drink my coffee? I only have a few minutes before I go back and relieve the first mate."

Charlotte wondered how he had entered the room without her being aware of it. His presence seemed to fill the space. She must have been really engrossed in that book, but now she couldn't even remember its title.

❧

Gareth hadn't intended to ask that last question. Even after his heart-to-heart with Doug and Homer over an early breakfast, he planned to keep his distance from this beautiful woman.

Although Doug encouraged him to develop a relationship with her, Homer agreed with Gareth that it wasn't a good idea. But here he was sitting across the table from her, and she looked like a reindeer caught in the headlights of a car. Large, luminous eyes with just a hint of fright in them. Why was she afraid? He wouldn't hurt her for the world. But he knew, even at this early stage, that she could hurt him if she wanted to.

"I see you had a good breakfast." Now why did he say that? "I mean, after not eating much of your dinner last night."

Charlotte's tense shoulders relaxed. "Yes, I was hungry. And the food is really good. You obviously have wonderful chefs aboard."

"Yes, over a hundred at last count."

She brushed dark curls back from her forehead. Gareth imagined his fingers tangled in those silky strands. The thought amazed him. When he carried on mild flirtations with women on cruises, he never touched them. At least not in that kind of way. He was very careful to keep everything light and. . .unentangled.

What was it about her that drew him? Last night when that other woman asked about her husband, he recognized the pain in her eyes. A shadow of it still lingered this morning. She was emotionally tied to her deceased husband. He knew all about such ties. Although it had been several years since Britte's death, he still loved his late wife very much.

Charlotte stood and started to gather her bag, sunglasses, and book. "I think I'll go see if I can find my daughter."

Gareth reached across the table and touched her arm. "Please don't leave just yet. I'm sure she's okay. There are crewmembers all over the ship to give passengers any help they need. Tell me a little about your family."

Charlotte sank back into the comfortable chair. "There isn't much to tell."

"Where are you from?" Gareth leaned his crossed arms on the small table.

"Texas. . .the Dallas-Fort Worth area." Charlotte hoped she looked all right. Her hair had fallen across her face while she was reading, and she had brushed it back several times. It probably looked like a rat's nest, and she knew she had eaten off all her lipstick. She gritted her teeth to keep from mashing her lips together to bring more color into them. Why did it matter? "Where are you from, Captain, uh. . .Gareth?"

❧

He liked the way his name rolled off her soft southern drawl. "I grew up in Belgium. But my family is from the Netherlands. My wife and I had a home in Oosterhout."

"Had?"

"Well, I still have the house, but Britte has been gone for over three years."

"Gone?"

It was a lame way to explain what happened. "Yes, she had cancer, but she hid it from me as long as she could. I spent her last nine months with her." Gareth couldn't believe he was telling her so much about his life. He never told anything personal to the women he spent time with on the cruises.

Charlotte reached over and patted his forearm. "I understand. Well, maybe I don't understand completely. Philip was killed by a drunk driver. It was sudden. I can't imagine watching your mate waste away for nine months." Tears pooled in her eyes, and a couple trailed down her cheeks.

Before she could wipe them off, Gareth gently touched her face. "Don't cry for me, Charlotte. I've learned to live with the pain."

"Maybe I'm crying for me as much as for you. I'm not sure I'll ever be able to really live with the pain." She dug in her purse and finally brought out an empty, crumpled tissue package.

Gareth reached into his back pocket and pulled out his handkerchief, glad that he'd put a fresh one in his trousers this morning. "Here." He took her chin in one hand and gently patted the fresh tears away.

As they gazed into each other's eyes, Gareth recognized a new understanding flowing between them. Maybe they could be friends for the length of the cruise. Then they would both move on.

❧

"Mom, where have you been?" When Charlotte opened the cabin door, Chelle stood in the middle of the room with her hands on her hips and wrapped in one of the large, thick bath towels.

"I could ask you the same thing." Charlotte closed the door and dropped her purse on the small table beside the couch. "You were gone when I got up."

"I went for a run around that top deck." She pulled a smaller towel from around her neck and began rubbing her wet hair. "When I got back, you were gone."

Charlotte picked up the day's itinerary from beside her bag. "There's a church service in the theater on deck four. Why don't we go?"

Chelle leaned toward the mirror above the desk and inspected her face, flicking at something on her cheek. "I haven't eaten yet." She turned back toward her mom. "Aren't you hungry?"

"I ate in the Oceanic Grille." Charlotte looked down at the itinerary. "It says here that we can call room service anytime.

Why don't we have something sent to the cabin for you? By the time it arrives, you should be dressed."

Charlotte could tell by the look on her daughter's face, this wouldn't have been her first choice, but she agreed.

❧

"Wow, Mom, this place is huge!" Chelle stood beside Charlotte at the back of the theater.

Before them, a carpeted aisle sloped downward toward the front. At this angle all the seats in the room must be good ones. Charlotte glanced around, trying to decide where to sit.

"You don't want to go down front, do you?" Chelle's question let her know what she thought.

"Where do you want to sit?" Might as well let her daughter make as many decisions as she could. Soon enough, something would come up where Charlotte would have to be the mother.

Chelle led the way, stopping a third of the way down the aisle. She moved into the row of seats and dropped into the second one. Good. She wanted to sit by the aisle. Charlotte did, too. Soft instrumental hymns played over the sound system, setting a tranquil mood. Most of the people in the room were several rows ahead of them. She wished they had chosen a place closer, but it didn't matter. She could worship wherever she was.

❧

"Mom, did you notice that the captain was at the church service?" Chelle dug through the clothes in her drawer, destroying the neat piles her mother created when she unpacked.

Charlotte set her Bible and purse on the table and reached down to pull off her high-heeled sandals. Why had she brought them? Even if they did look good, she was on vacation, and they definitely weren't comfortable for long. "Yes, I noticed him sitting over to the side."

"I think it's cool that the captain is a Christian." Chelle pulled some bits of fabric from the middle of her favorite beach towel.

"Just because he was there doesn't mean he's a Christian." But Charlotte hoped he was. Surely she wouldn't feel so drawn to a man who wasn't.

"I know." Chelle pulled her T-shirt over her head. "But I saw him singing the praise songs, and he wasn't reading the words on the screens. It looked to me like he was worshiping."

Charlotte moved through the hangers in the closet, trying to decide what to wear for the rest of the day. Maybe the navy capris and white T-shirt with the stylized American flag design on the front. She turned around and frowned.

"What are you doing?"

Chelle's defiant eyes glared at her. "I'm going out to get some sun. Maybe by the pool on deck nine."

"Not in that, you're not." Charlotte tried not to sound too strident. "Where did you get that bikini?"

"Merry loaned it to me." Chelle started rubbing suntan lotion on her exposed stomach. "She said I'd need it on a cruise."

Charlotte counted to ten under her breath. What she wanted to do was get her hands on Merry. The girl was nice enough, but her parents' standards and discipline were looser than Charlotte's and Philip's had always been.

"You are not going out of this room dressed like that."

"M–o–m." Chelle took a deep breath. "I'm not doing anything bad."

Charlotte hated this—this frequent battle between the generations. If only she had someone to back her up. At times like these, Philip's absence grew enormous.

"I know you aren't going to do anything bad, but we've

talked often enough about how what you do affects others."

Chelle started saying the words with her, and Charlotte's voice trailed off. "Other people judge you by what you do and wear. You don't want them to get the wrong idea. And you don't want to tempt a young man to sin."

They stood staring at each other, locked in stalemate.

"Are you telling me I have to wear something else?"

Charlotte nodded, almost too upset to say anything. "Remember, we did buy you a new swimsuit to bring on the cruise." She picked up the two-piece with a tank-style top and boy-leg shorts.

Chelle gave a loud huff. Did she think she would wear her mother down and Charlotte would agree to those tiny patches of fabric that left nothing to the imagination? Didn't she see what a beautiful young woman she was becoming? *Lord, I need Your help and wisdom, now more than ever.*

While Chelle changed, Charlotte looked over the list of excursions. Maybe it would help diffuse the tension in the room. "This brochure says we need to choose which of these we want to go on and order the tickets today. Some of them might fill up quickly." She sat on the couch and slipped on her flat sandals. "Have you decided what you want to do at our first stop, Cozumel?"

"Yes, I want to go to the Tulum ruins and Xel-Ha. That really is a funny way to spell shell."

Charlotte leafed through the book. "That's a long excursion— eight hours away from the ship. I don't think I want to be gone that long. Maybe we could do something else."

Chelle heaved an exaggerated sigh. "Do we have to do everything together?" She stopped and tried another tack. "If I promise not to ask to wear this again"—she held up the bikini—"can I go?"

Compromise. That's the way to do it. Charlotte was glad for an end to the argument about the inappropriate swimsuit.

"I'm sure they won't let anything happen to the people who go, and since I'm old enough to work, I should be able to take care of myself on the excursion." Chelle gave Charlotte a hopeful smile.

Charlotte paused, then decided she could give on this one. "Okay, I'll sign you up. We can talk about the excursions on Grand Cayman and Jamaica later." She didn't want to have another hassle right now.

After Chelle left the cabin, Charlotte decided to explore some of the ship. Coming on the trip with her daughter had sounded like a good idea, but it looked as if she would be spending a lot of solitary time, too. Their interests were different, and Chelle didn't want her mother hanging around all the time. If they went to the shows together and ate most meals with each other, maybe they would both enjoy the trip.

On the elevator, a woman asked where Charlotte was from. The woman spoke with a thick accent. Charlotte tried to place it. "We're from Bedford, Texas. Where do you live?"

"Germany." The woman's friendly smile warmed Charlotte's heart.

"Did you come over just for the cruise?"

"Jah, we came for cruise, but we spent two nights in French Quarter of New Orleans before we got on boat."

Charlotte exited the elevator and looked all around the Centrum, the four-deck-high atrium with balcony railings on each of the decks. Her eyes roved the wall of windows on each side of deck four. All she could see was water and the sky with a few cottony clouds. She almost felt as if she were on the ark. Nothing but water everywhere. At least the accommodations were luxurious, and there weren't any smelly animals.

After exploring the other decks surrounding the Centrum, she went back to deck seven to check out the library. Since she liked to read, it beckoned her. A large room, which could be divided into two, held welcoming furniture groupings, and many of the walls were lined with bookshelves. Warm, rich wood and lots of brass complemented the pulled-back drapes and forest green carpet. Even with all this, Charlotte felt the openness of the room, because the outside wall consisted of floor-to-ceiling windows, and the wall that faced the Centrum was all glass, letting in the outside world.

Charlotte walked along the bookshelves to see what was available. An interesting and eclectic collection of reading material spread across the polished wooden shelves. A couple of sections held books that passengers had left for others. She glanced through them and found one by her favorite author of Christian suspense. A title she hadn't read yet. She picked the volume up and thumbed through it. Maybe she'd take it for those leisure times when she didn't want to do anything but relax and read.

She chose a chair that faced the ocean and read the back cover. Goose bumps raised on her arms. Maybe she wouldn't relax that much when she read this one, but it was the last one in a series. She had read the first two.

Charlotte sensed the door open and glanced over her shoulder. Her gaze collided with that of the captain. . .Gareth.

❧

Gareth often took a break from the bridge, especially while they were at sea. Homer was perfectly capable of taking care of things, and while they were moving across open water, frequent breaks were called for to keep from getting bored, losing their edge, and missing something important they should have caught.

His restlessness sent him to the library. Perhaps one of the passengers had left a book he hadn't read. Next time they were in New Orleans, he planned to visit a bookstore and restock his supply of reading material.

As he approached the glass walls of the library, he noticed a seated woman. She faced away from the door. From the back, it looked like Charlotte. What good luck. Even though he didn't seek her out at the service this morning, she had been in his thoughts a lot since then. A short visit right now would be a good thing.

She turned toward him, and her startled gaze reached deep inside him. "Charlotte, how nice to see you again." How lame was that?

"Capt–Gareth. . .do you like to read?"

He quickly dropped into the chair beside hers. "Yes. Although we have satellite TV, many of the shows don't interest me. I enjoy reading."

"Something else we have in common."

Did she know how that sounded? As if she were looking for a connection between them. Well, so was he now. But only a light, shipboard romance. He couldn't face another relationship that could cut him to the core the way the last months with Britte had done. No more loving so much and giving his heart, only to have it broken and bruised.

"What are you reading?" His gaze dropped to the cover of the book.

"It's a Christian suspense novel. I love reading suspense and mystery, but so many of the books had things I didn't like to read." Her smile lit the whole room. "I'm glad to find more and more Christian suspense books."

"Did you bring it with you?"

She laid the book in her lap. "No, I got it off your exchange shelf over there. I've read the other two in this series."

"I've found several good books on those shelves." He leaned forward with his forearms on his thighs. "Maybe I can read it if you finish it before we dock in New Orleans."

"You mean I can take it home with me if I don't?" Mirth put a crinkle around her eyes, making her face soften. She looked much younger.

He nodded. "So, what have you been doing today? I mean besides going to the service."

"So you did notice us there." She sure sounded glad. "Chelle and I were trying to decide what excursions to take. She wants to go to Tulum and Xel-Ha. I don't think I want to spend that much time on an excursion. I may want to do a little shopping."

By her tone, something was bothering her. "Is there a problem?"

"I told her she could go alone, but I can't help worrying." She started twisting a lock of her shoulder-length curls with her right hand. "I can't have anything happen to her."

He heard the *too* she left unsaid at the end of that statement, and his heart softened at her vulnerability. "She'll be okay. The crewmembers who accompany the group watch out for the passengers. They're well trained." Maybe a joke would lighten the atmosphere in here. "We haven't lost a passenger yet."

Charlotte gave a nervous laugh. "Isn't this only the second cruise for this ship?"

She had him there. "But most of the crew members have been there several times. They've served on other ships owned by the line. Only the most experienced and responsible members of the crew go on an excursion like that." He took her hand and gazed deep into her eyes. "Nothing will happen to your daughter on my watch."

❧

After his leisurely hour break, Gareth returned to his quarters. He called Doug immediately. "Who do you have going to Tulum and Xel-Ha tomorrow?"

The purser rattled off a list of crewmembers with the most experience with this kind of tour. "What's this all about? These are the ones who usually go."

"Chelle Halloran wants to go, but her mother doesn't. Charlotte's almost afraid to let her go, but she did buy her a ticket. Could you assign someone to keep a special eye on her without her knowing it?"

After a long pause, Doug answered, "I'll take care of it for you. . .Gareth, do you know what you're doing? I know I told you I thought a pretty lady might do you some good, but don't move too fast."

"It's nothing to worry about. I'm just giving a passenger a little personal attention. I've done it before, and you've never said anything."

"Sure you have. But not like this time."

Gareth ended the call before his friend could say something else. He was just doing a favor for a friend. That's all, wasn't it?

three

At 5 a.m., the phone rang with the wake-up call for Chelle. Of course she didn't hear it, so Charlotte hurried across the carpet to answer. Then she shook her daughter until Chelle finally groaned and opened her eyes.

"You were the one who wanted to go on this excursion that leaves at six." Charlotte dropped a quick kiss on Chelle's forehead. Opportunities to kiss her teenager were few and far between. Better get one now, while she was so groggy.

Chelle made her way to the shower, carrying shampoo and conditioner. Charlotte went back to bed and turned over, trying to go to sleep. Even though she dozed, she heard every sound her daughter made as she showered, dried her hair, put on her makeup, and tried on at least three outfits before she was ready. When the door clicked shut behind the teenager, Charlotte hoped sleep would come.

After tossing and turning for almost half an hour, she got up and dressed. Today she would try breakfast in the dining room. Since seating wasn't assigned except at dinner, she decided to try another section of the beautiful space. As she walked toward an empty table, the tall German woman she met in the elevator the day before waved to her.

"Come sit here."

At least she didn't have to eat alone. After the waiter pushed in her chair and put the napkin in her lap, Charlotte held out her hand to her breakfast companion. "I am Charlotte Halloran."

The woman gave Charlotte's hand a vigorous shake. "Gertrud Bergmann." She wore her short blond hair swept back on the sides but with curls on top.

"Have you already ordered, Gertrud?" Charlotte glanced over the menu, trying to make up her mind.

"I'm about ready. So many things to choose from."

The waiter hovered a short distance from the table, probably waiting for them to let him know they needed him. Charlotte glanced his way, and he came over.

"Has Madame decided what to eat?"

⁂

When Charlotte bought the ticket for Chelle, she bought herself one for the Cozumel Highlights tour. Several crew-members herded the group out the doorway onto the dock almost half an hour before the bus was scheduled to leave. After leaving the ship, each passenger or group of passengers had to stop behind a COZUMEL sign so one of the ship's photographers could take a picture. Charlotte stood there alone, wondering if she would even be interested in this one. She and Chelle had looked at the pictures taken on the first day of the cruise, but she wanted to wait and choose only the best ones to buy. The problem was, every one of the pictures flattered both of them.

By the time the group finally boarded the bus, they were about ten minutes behind schedule. Charlotte hoped that wasn't how the day would progress. She settled back against the seat, which felt much narrower than any bus she had been on back home. Maybe all that good food had already started changing the shape of her body. She glanced back toward the ship. It looked beautiful tied up beside a long wooden dock with the turquoise Caribbean Sea behind it framing the stark white of the exterior. She wondered how they kept it so clean.

And the color of the water here was so different from the gulf water they crossed yesterday. Her gaze was drawn toward the bridge one last time. A man stood outside the doorway. From this distance, she couldn't tell who it was. Gareth, perhaps.

⁂

Gareth stood on the tiny balcony beside the bridge, watching the passengers leave. Doug told him at breakfast that Charlotte had bought a ticket on the island tour. How long had it been since he went ashore in Cozumel? His last ship visited there only every other week, so it had to be a year or more, but he remembered everything about the island. The tall palm trees, the areas of jungle, snow-white beaches against the vivid blue waters, older homes, resorts, the sleepy fishing villages that had evolved into shopping meccas. Why did he feel a yearning to see it all again?

The next group of passengers disembarked with Charlotte in the midst. Today her hair was pulled up into a short ponytail, and a red sun visor hid her eyes from his view. Gareth could have put himself on the schedule to be away from the ship today. Why hadn't he?

Because he wasn't going to get really involved with any woman. Especially one who tugged at his heart the way Charlotte did. He watched her stop for the picture. . .alone. Most of the people on the tour at least had a partner or friend with them. Gareth imagined himself standing beside her and having their picture taken. He would have gone in civilian clothes, not the uniform of a ship captain. For one day, he could be just a friend.

As Charlotte walked down the dock then up the paved path toward the buses, he studied her. At least she had the good sense to wear enough clothing that she wouldn't get burned. The sun beat stronger this close to the equator. It would be a shame for her soft skin to be damaged.

She was the picture of every Christian man's ideal woman. Okay, maybe not every man's, but she looked ideal to him.

Gareth knew he must have lost his mind. What was he doing watching her? All it did was cause him to want things. Things that would never be part of his life again. Things that brought an ache to his heart. But, he didn't draw his gaze away until the bus pulled out of the parking lot and headed down the street that ran along beside the island's seawall.

The ship wasn't going anywhere. Maybe Gareth should go to his apartment and. . .do what? What was he going to do all day while she toured the island? He picked up the schedule to see where it would end.

❧

Around one o'clock, the bus stopped in a parking lot about a block from the street that ran between the shops and the beaches. Charlotte waited until everyone else had crowded into the aisle and most of them had left the bus. She picked up her tote bag and headed toward the front of the vehicle. When she started down the steps, a masculine hand stretched toward her. As she grasped it, she was poised on the last long step to the stones that covered the parking lot. A tingle shot up her arm, and she turned her eyes toward the man's face. A familiar smile touched her heart, but she wouldn't have recognized him if he hadn't taken her hand. She had thought the uniform was dashing, but without it, he was even more devastatingly handsome. Her heart skipped a beat.

"Hello, Charlotte, did you enjoy the tour?"

"Gareth, what are you doing here? And where is your uniform?" She knew that was a dumb question, but she had to scramble to collect her scattered wits. Thankfully, the other passengers hurried away from the area.

"Let's just say I'm taking some time off from being captain of the ship." He pulled her hand through his arm, and they strolled down the shaded street. "What did you plan to do the rest of the day?"

She tore her gaze from his and looked around. They were headed away from where the stores lined the street. "I thought I might do some shopping."

Gareth wheeled them around and started to walk in the other direction. "Have you had lunch?"

"No, and I'm hungry." A breeze off the water blew down the canyon created by the buildings, bringing welcome coolness. However, she felt hotter than she had in the unair-conditioned bus.

He turned down the sidewalk in front of the shops and moved to the side nearer the street. "I know just the place. They serve excellent seafood and Mexican specialties."

Charlotte felt protected by his chivalry. She smiled up at him. "Is it safe to eat there?"

"I wouldn't take you anywhere that wasn't completely safe." His eyes twinkled. "We can even drink the water. The proprietor is proud of the fact that he uses Culligan water in his establishment."

Over lunch, Charlotte began to relax. With his tropical shirt and khaki walking shorts, Gareth lost his authoritative air. He was just a man. . .a friend. . .sharing a meal with her.

"Did you like the show last night?" Gareth had finished eating a rather large steak and now leaned back in his chair.

The show last night? For a moment, Charlotte had to think about that. "Yes, it was refreshing to have a comedian who was so funny and yet I didn't have to worry about what my daughter heard. Were you there?"

Gareth leaned closer. "No. I heard him last week." The

room was noisy. Maybe he had a hard time hearing her. "Our line will only book acts that keep it clean. We cater to families as well as adults."

⋟⋞

Now why did I say that? I sounded like a travel brochure. Gareth could easily lose himself in her eyes. Today, for a while, the pain was absent. Charlotte had relaxed enough to have fun.

"Didn't you say you want to do some shopping?" He pushed back his chair and stood up, reaching to pull out hers. "What did you have in mind?"

She searched in the large bag she carried and extracted several pieces of paper. They were some of the ones the shopper's guide on the ship handed out. "I'd like to go to Del Sol and see about some of the things that change color in the sun. I also like Mexican clothing. Maybe look at a leather purse."

They headed toward the door. "Don't you want to look at the jewelry?"

"Isn't the jewelry shopping better on Grand Cayman?" The expression on her face as she looked up hit him in the solar plexus.

He casually slipped his arm around her shoulders. At least he hoped the move felt casual to her. "The jewelry on Grand Cayman is fine jewelry. Here you get a selection of fun kinds, too. Let me show you."

Gareth guided her toward his favorite store. Almost like a department store in the United States, this one contained many kinds of merchandise. They wandered through the aisles. Near the front door, jewelry cases lined one side of the *tienda*. Charlotte walked along, looking at the sparkling merchandise, and Gareth looked at her.

She stopped where the jeweler had fashioned gold into

seashells and mounted pearls in the shells. Necklaces and earring sets, as well as individual items, spread from side to side in this glass case. Charlotte had the merchant bring out several pieces, one at a time. She kept going back to one pair of earrings but finally shook her head and walked on. The older Mexican man started to say something, but Gareth signaled him to stop. The man moved on to the next customer.

Following Charlotte as she found the clothing, Gareth stayed close enough to help her if she needed it, but far enough away not to bother her. She picked out several things she wanted to try on.

"Take your time." Gareth chuckled. "I'll just wander around until you're through. I might find something I want."

"Thank you." With a saucy smile, she entered the dressing area curtained off in the back corner of the room.

Gareth hastened back to the jewelry counter. The other customer had moved on. He called the proprietor over and bought the earrings Charlotte kept going back to earlier. After slipping the box into his pocket, he did what he told her he would do and wandered around the store, keeping one eye on the doorway to the dressing room.

When Charlotte came out, she kept most of the things she took in. He would have quite a few packages to carry back to the ship for her. She continued around the store, picking out a couple of Cozumel T-shirts and two leather purses.

After she paid for her purchases, Gareth gathered the packages and held out his other arm. "Did you want to do any more shopping?"

She clutched his elbow. "Actually, I'm pretty tired. With the humidity, it seems hotter than it really is. When does the bus go back to the ship?"

"Your chariot awaits."

They walked to the street corner closest to them. Gareth signaled to the man who was in charge of the taxis lined up on the other side of the street from the shops. At the first break in the traffic, he escorted Charlotte across the cobblestones. A taxi waited with its motor running. He helped Charlotte into the backseat. After giving her all her packages, he started toward the other side.

When he went around the front of the car, Gareth leaned toward the driver's open window and whispered. "There's an extra ten for you if you'll turn the air-conditioning on high and roll up the windows." By the time Gareth got in and closed his door, colder air blew into the compact car.

❧

When they reached the dock, the taxi let them out at a different place from where she had boarded the bus. This area had lots of shops.

"Where's the ship?" Charlotte asked after they gathered everything out of the taxi.

"On the other side of these shops." This time, Gareth reached for her hand and didn't let go.

How could she have forgotten how good it felt? Warm, gentle pressure engulfed her hand, making her feel safe and protected. That's how she'd felt with Gareth the entire time they were in town. On the tour, she had felt lonely, but not now.

"I think taxis stop here so passengers will be enticed to buy something else before they board the ship." Gareth's expression questioned her. "Do you want to go into any of the shops?"

She glanced around. Even though the establishment held many interesting items, she wasn't tempted. "No, let's just go onboard. I feel hot and tired." She followed him as he led the way through the vendors vying for their attention. "But at least the taxi ride started cooling me off."

They quickly navigated toward the dock. The interior of the vessel seemed dim when they came in out of the bright sunlight. The crewman who manned the security point glanced from her to Gareth before he asked for her room key. Charlotte wished she had been looking at Gareth to see his reaction, but he didn't let her hand go until she had to dig in her bag to retrieve the card. She had to step up to the machine, and it scanned her face.

"Okay, welcome aboard, Mrs. Halloran."

The young man smiled at her and motioned her to step to the next station. There all the packages had to go on a conveyor belt and through an X-ray machine, much like the ones at the airport.

Gareth leaned closer. "Before nine-eleven, we didn't have to do all this. You go on past the machine, and I'll put the bags on the belt. You can watch them come through."

Charlotte did as he said. When they boarded the elevator, no one joined them.

"I don't usually go to passengers' cabins. Will you be all right with these packages?"

"Of course." She started taking them from him, wedging them under her arms. "It will feel good to clean up and change clothes."

The car stopped, but Gareth pushed the button that kept the door closed. "There are elevators closer to the front of the ship. Please meet me at those on deck seven in an hour."

Something in his tone touched Charlotte. "Okay. I'll be there."

❧

Gareth paced from his apartment to the elevator and back. Through the open door to Homer's quarters, which shared a wall with his, Gareth saw his first mate look up from the newspaper he was reading.

"Are you nervous?" His friend's voice called.

Before he could formulate an answer, the bell on the elevator down the hall dinged. He turned and hurried toward it, reaching the small lobby as the doors slid open.

Charlotte stepped out and looked around. Her eyes lit up when she saw him. "There you are." She came toward him, wearing another of those soft cloudy dresses that swirled around her trim figure. "Where are we going?"

He ushered her down the corridor in front of him. "To the captain's quarters. I thought you might like to see them."

She stopped just before she reached the two side-by-side open doors. She slowly turned and looked stricken. "I'm not sure that's a good idea."

The whispered words cut to Gareth's heart. What did she think he wanted?

"This must be the lovely Mrs. Halloran." Homer leaned against his doorjamb, and Charlotte glanced toward him. "I'm sure the captain was planning to introduce us, but I couldn't wait." He took one of Charlotte's hands. "Homer Wilson, first mate, at your service, ma'am." He gave a slight bow.

Gareth moved around them in the narrow hallway. "I wanted you to see where we live the three months we are on the ship."

Charlotte pulled her hand from Homer's, and none too soon, Gareth thought.

"Three months?"

Gareth took her elbow and pulled her toward the living room in his suite. "Yes, the first mate and I spend three months on the ship, then three months at home."

A tall woman with straight brown hair came to the door

of Homer's cabin, drying her hands on a towel. "This time Homer is staying six months, so I came to be with him for a while." She dropped the towel on a chair near the door and stuck out her hand. "I'm Marilyn Wilson, and I've wanted to meet you ever since Homer told me about you."

Gareth cringed. He hoped that didn't scare Charlotte off. "Come in. I want to give her a tour." After looking out the windows of the living room, which spread across half the front of the ship and down the side, he led the group into his office.

"What are all those charts on the wall?" Charlotte walked over and squinted as if she were trying to read the tiny print. "Do you use them for navigation?"

Gareth moved closer behind her. "Most of that is done using computers and satellites, but I still like to have the charts to look at. On some of the ships I've captained, they have kept us out of a few jams."

Marilyn stood at the door. "I've made us some refreshments, if you have time to visit." They went next door where a tray of desserts and coffee sat on the table in front of the couch.

After they had eaten and chatted for a few minutes, Charlotte asked, "Do you get many foreign passengers on the cruises? I had breakfast this morning with a woman from Germany."

"Yes, cruises are popular with people from all around the world." Gareth turned toward Homer. "Do you remember how many countries are represented this time?"

"I was just looking at the list." He rubbed his forehead above his eyes. "Let's see, there are some from Brazil, Mexico, Germany, Japan, Canada, and the Philippines. That's just the passengers. If you look closely at each crewmember's name badge, you can see where they are from. Over forty countries, I think."

❧

When Charlotte arrived back at her cabin, Chelle stood holding another white envelope. "We've been invited to eat at the captain's table again this evening. I thought he invited different people each night."

Charlotte didn't like her tone, but she didn't want to spoil the day with another disagreement. "Maybe not. How was your day?"

All during the time they got ready to go to dinner, Chelle regaled her with tales of the ruins, the swimming at Xel-Ha, the people she met, and the crewmembers who accompanied them. Seeing her so happy gladdened Charlotte's heart.

When they arrived in the dining room, the only person they knew was the captain, and he saved places for Charlotte and Chelle beside him. Once again, the variety of food, and its quality and uniqueness, astounded Charlotte. The kitchens had to be large to accommodate all the chefs and helpers. Maybe she would ask Gareth the next time they were alone together.

This time, all the people lingered over dessert and coffee, sharing about how they spent the day. Another newlywed couple ate dinner with them, and they drank a whole bottle of champagne. Charlotte wasn't sure she wanted Chelle being around them, but they left the table before anyone else.

"Mother, isn't it time we went to our cabins to get ready for the show?" Chelle pushed her chair back and stood.

Charlotte did the same. "Okay. We can go." She turned to those still seated at the table and Gareth who stood behind his chair. "We've enjoyed this time with you, haven't we, Chelle?"

The noncommittal teenage grunt and look in her eyes warned Charlotte that her daughter was upset about something. She was sure she'd find out soon enough.

She was right. The cabin door barely closed behind them when Chelle turned on her. "What's going on, Mother?" She didn't sound like the whiny teenager who could stretch the word Mom so far. Charlotte wasn't ready for her daughter to sound so grown up.

"I'm not sure what you're talking about." Charlotte reached for the itinerary for the next day, hoping Chelle would take the hint that she didn't want to discuss it.

"You and that captain. He couldn't take his eyes off you, and you were eating up the attention." She spat the words as if they tasted bad.

They poured over Charlotte like bitter acid. Did the other people see it that way? Had she been indiscreet?

"Gar—Captain Van den Hout was a perfect host and a gentleman."

Chelle stomped across the floor then kicked off her platform sandals. Charlotte hoped the sound didn't carry to the deck below them. "You are so naive, Mother. That man has the hots for you."

Charlotte couldn't believe what her daughter had said. "Chelle, where did you hear things like that?"

"I am not a baby, and I know what's going on."

Charlotte had a hard time holding her anger in check. "Nothing's going on."

"How could you forget Daddy like that?" Chelle threw herself down on the bed and sobs tore through her. After a moment, she asked without turning her head, "Don't you love him anymore?"

Charlotte sat beside her and reached to touch her, but Chelle moved away. "Of course, I love your father. You're reading things into the situation that aren't there."

Chelle got up and started undressing. "I don't want to talk about this. I'm tired. . .I'm going to bed."

"What about the show?"

"You go if you want to." Chelle's petulant tone hurt her mother. "I don't want to anymore."

While Chelle moved around the cabin throwing things down and jerking her pajamas on, Charlotte quietly prepared to retire, too. Long after soft snores came from her daughter, Charlotte lay in her bed thinking. What was she doing? This man did disturb her, but her daughter had not gotten over losing Philip, and neither had she. Time with Gareth was courting danger. Danger to their family and danger to her heart. She was not going to spend any more time with the man.

four

When Chelle woke up, Charlotte was thankful her daughter's mood had lightened. Chelle was so much like her daddy, who ignored problems, thinking they would just go away. Charlotte decided to implement her plan to spend quality time with her daughter. While Chelle carefully applied more makeup than she usually wore, Charlotte perused the list of excursions. She knew she should call her daughter on the excessive makeup, but she didn't want to ruin the day so early.

"We've waited pretty late to buy our excursion tickets for today. What do you want to do? Maybe they'll still have a few available."

Chelle turned around. "I want to go see the stingrays. Maybe go snorkeling with them."

Charlotte picked up the phone and punched the numbers for the purser's desk. "Do you still have tickets for the Stingray and Snorkeling excursion? . . . You do? We need two of them. I'll come up and get them before breakfast."

"Let me run this through the computer." The voice sounded like the cute young woman Charlotte met when she got their earlier tickets.

The smile fell off Chelle's face. "M–o–m! We don't have to do everything together."

Here we go again. Charlotte covered the mouthpiece of the phone, but kept it near her ear. "I thought we'd do something together today."

Chelle put down her mascara with more force than necessary. "We can have breakfast and dinner together." She picked up lip gloss and started unscrewing the thin, shiny tube. "Maybe we can go to the show tonight."

She left unsaid the reason they didn't go last night, and Charlotte didn't want to bring that subject up either.

"I'm sorry, Mrs. Halloran, but we only have one ticket for that excursion. Would you want to order tickets to something else?"

Maybe if she gave on this one, the peace would be worth it. "Okay, we'll take that one. How about another ticket to the Butterfly farm and Nautilus mini-submarine?"

"Yes, actually we have two left for that trip. Do you want both of them?"

Chelle watched her mother, waiting for her to continue, almost as if she heard the other end of the phone conversation.

"We'll take one of each." Charlotte watched her daughter let out the breath she had been holding.

"We can have them sent to your room. They'll be there when you return from breakfast."

"Thank you."

Chelle's grin rewarded Charlotte for the decision she made. Charlotte replaced the earpiece of the phone and returned her smile. "So where do you want to have breakfast?" Maybe when they both got back from the trips, they could do something together on the ship.

❧

A spectacular tropical garden inhabited by butterflies from around the world spread out before Charlotte. Sights and smells overwhelmed her senses. Color bursts of fluttering wings that settled on delicate blossoms then lifted off to find another resting place provided a kaleidoscopic atmosphere.

The heady essence of orchids, birds of paradise, and other exotic flowers created a perfume unparalleled, even by the most expensive names in fragrance. God's blending was perfect. Charlotte wished they could bottle it and sell it. She would choose it as her signature perfume.

While she enjoyed the lavishness of the setting, she forgot to feel lonely. Everyone else on the excursion had one or more partners to share it with, so riding on the bus across the island, she felt alone. When she boarded the return bus, the loneliness fell on her again like a wet blanket, making the hot air hard to breathe. She didn't even want to think about what the cruise would be like if Philip were with her. She would not go there. But sharing this with her daughter, or her own best friend back home, would have made the day even better.

When they reached the submarine, Charlotte hung back, letting the groups be seated together. She'd just take whatever place was left. After sinking onto the thinly padded seat covered with plastic upholstery, she felt as if she were taking part in some science fiction book or movie. She always liked reading Jules Verne when she was younger, and this submarine felt like something out of one of his books.

"We'll leave in just a few minutes," said the perky young man who would serve as their guide. He held a clipboard on which he had ticked off the name of each person who boarded. "We have one more passenger who is running a little late."

Charlotte had counted everyone on the bus over to the gardens and on the way over here from there. Maybe it went back to the times she served as a room mother and accompanied field trips. Counting children kept them from the catastrophe of leaving one behind. Everyone had been on the second bus. She looked around and counted the people in the sub again. They were all here. She started once again, in case she miscounted. Before she finished, a man in navy shorts and a white polo shirt with thin navy stripes across his muscular chest climbed down the ladder and slipped into the seat beside her.

"Hello, Charlotte. Surprised to see me?"

Surprised didn't even describe this feeling that coursed through her. Happy. . .unsettled. . .she could think of a lot of words that better explained the shiver that skittered down her spine.

"Capt–Gareth, are you taking time off again today?" Of course he was, or he wouldn't be here beside her. So much for her decision not to spend time with him again.

ॐ

"Yes." What else could he add to that?

The guide closed the hatch, and the sub pulled away from the dock, slowly sinking below the surface of the water. The young man started his spiel. Gareth had heard it all before. Personally, he preferred floating on top of the waves in a larger craft to being held captive below the surface in this thing, but the chance to spend more time with Charlotte made the trip worth it.

He watched expressions chase themselves across her face. It was like watching a movie, and he recognized each of her feelings. Something bothered her, and he wanted to find out what. He felt a strong desire to fix it for her. Maybe it had something to do with Chelle. She hadn't seemed very happy at dinner last night. Had something happened after they left the dining room? Something that kept the two women from attending the show? Gareth had gone to the lighting booth in the theater, hoping to catch a glimpse of Charlotte, but he couldn't see her sitting anywhere in the large room. He wanted to watch them as they enjoyed the unusual act.

Charlotte's gaze stayed glued to the guide. She obediently looked each direction he indicated, searching the ocean floor for the items the man referenced. Finally, she peeked sideways, up at Gareth's face. He smiled, hoping to put her at ease. Maybe this wasn't such a good idea. He shouldn't have made Doug tell him where she was going. Although Gareth had missed the butterflies, he'd made it to the sub.

"I'm glad to see you again." Her whispered words pulled him from his thoughts.

Drawn into the blue depths, he couldn't take his eyes off of hers. "Me, too." Once again, the guide's voice intruded, and Gareth glanced toward the window. "Look over there, Charlotte." He reached around her and pointed to a rough, bumpy lump surrounded by waving, wide-leafed aquatic plants on the ocean floor. "There's a giant conch." She peered down, and he left his arm across the back of the seat they shared.

"My grandmother had one of those shells she used as a doorstop." Her voice contained a wistful note.

"The island natives make a wonderful soup with the meat from conchs."

She turned startled eyes toward him. "They eat them?"

"They're just another shellfish. Most things living in the oceans are edible."

The guide pointed out a shipwreck half buried in the coral reef. He spouted the history of the wooden ship and its occupants. Charlotte sat spellbound, taking it all in. Maybe she was as interested in history as Gareth was. That would be something else they could discuss when they spent time together.

After they reached Cheeseburger Reef, a guide swimming in

the water fed the fish right outside their window. The multi-colored fish crowding close to the window held Charlotte's complete attention. This allowed Gareth to study her at leisure. Long lashes fringed her bright blue eyes, which sparkled with excitement. The sun had kissed her skin enough to give it a golden glow, but without burning it. She looked vital and alive. With her hair once again pulled into that short ponytail, she could pass as a slightly older sister of Chelle's. That question he asked her the first night didn't sound so lame now.

❧

When the majority of the bright fish moved down the side of the vessel, Charlotte realized that Gareth was watching her instead of the sea creatures. A blush warmed her cheeks. Maybe he would just think she was sunburned or overheated. She was overheated, but it wasn't from the sun. It was from his presence so close to her. *What am I doing, responding to a man like this? It must be the romantic atmosphere of a cruise.* When they returned to Bedford, hopefully she would regain her sanity. She glanced up at Gareth.

"Are you enjoying yourself, Charlotte?" His crisp Oxford English contained a hint of another accent, probably Dutch.

"It's wonderful." She picked up her tote bag from the floor and held it in her lap. "I didn't realize how much is buried on the floor of the Caribbean."

"There's history all around you wherever you are." His smile made his eyes twinkle. A lock of curly blond hair had fallen against the top of his forehead, giving him a rakish air. "What eras are most interesting to you?"

His question helped her relax. Talking about the past was a safe way to spend the rest of the afternoon.

When they arrived back at the dock, Gareth helped her up, and they were the first to exit the underwater vessel since they were closest to the ladder. A taxi waited beside the bus, with its engine running. Gareth took her hand and pulled her toward the car. Although most of the vehicles on the island had their windows open, the driver had the windows rolled up. Charlotte settled gladly into the welcome coolness. The ride back to the ship only took a few minutes.

They arrived at the same time as the tender that took the snorkelers to Stingray City. The passengers on that boat were stepping up on the dock when the taxi stopped at the end of the paved lane that led to the ship. Charlotte glanced toward the dock in time to see Chelle. Although she had one of the large towels provided by the cruise line stuffed into her beach bag, she should have been using it to cover the tiny bikini Charlotte had forbidden her to wear.

Charlotte stiffened. Gareth noticed, because he turned questioning eyes her direction. She didn't want to pull him into the discussion, so she tried to relax. It took all the effort she could muster. Gareth looked past her toward the entrance to the ship. Charlotte hoped he didn't see her daughter flaunting herself in front of those young men on her excursion. Just wait until she got to the cabin.

Once again, they had to go through security. By the time the snorkelers were out of the way, the other people from the Butterfly and Nautilus trip were in line ahead of Charlotte.

"That was fun." She tried to sound bright and carefree.

From the expression on Gareth's face, it didn't work, but he didn't question her. At least it didn't take long to get everything scanned, since they hadn't been shopping. When Charlotte picked up her tote bag and turned around, the other passengers were gone. Gareth walked her to the elevator.

"Charlotte, I look forward to the next time we are together."

She nodded. The warmth in his eyes couldn't thaw the cold

knot that had settled in her chest. How she longed to be able to relax and enjoy her short time with this man, but when she got to the cabin, she would have to confront Chelle.

After sliding her key card into the slot, Charlotte pushed the door open. Chelle was taking a shower. Usually, she left the clothes she removed all over the floor when she did that, but even though Charlotte looked all around, she couldn't see the offending bathing suit. She slipped her tote bag onto the table and sat on the end of the couch.

What am I going to do about Chelle? I can't let her think that what she's doing is okay. I hope I can keep from losing my temper.

The water shut off, and Charlotte leaned her head back. Tension gripped her neck and shoulders. She took a deep breath and tried to relax. Even manually trying to relax each muscle group didn't work. When she moved to the next, the last one tightened again.

Charlotte got up and paced to the window. The steward had pulled the heavy drapes to the sides when he cleaned the room, but Charlotte took hold of the sheer curtain, which didn't part in the middle, and pushed it to one side. She stared at the end of the island visible from their stateroom. Life out there didn't touch what was happening in here. People went about their business, completely disconnected from the passengers on the cruise ship. The tourists were only a way to make a living for most of the natives.

The bathroom door opened. "Mom, you're back."

Charlotte didn't turn around. She kept looking at the tropical paradise in front of her. "Where is it, Chelle?"

"Where's what?" She sounded as if she didn't know what her mom was talking about. She probably didn't know that Charlotte had seen her.

Finally, Charlotte turned. "The bikini. Where is it?"

For a moment, Chelle paled then her face flushed. "I'm going to take it back to Merry."

"Give it to me, Chelle." At Charlotte's steely tone, her daughter took a step backward.

The teenager went to her large drawer and pawed through the clothes in it. "It should be right here, but I can't find it."

"Is it still wet?" Charlotte walked closer to her daughter.

"Wet?" Chelle licked her lips and took a deep breath. "I don't think it's wet."

Charlotte glanced down at the carpet then back at her daughter. "Have you been out of the water long enough for it to dry out?"

Tears filled Chelle's eyes. "How"—her voice had a catch in it—"how did you know?"

Holding out her hand, Charlotte answered, "I saw you get out of the boat." Then she lost her control on her anger. "What did you think you were doing parading around almost naked in front of those hormonal young men?"

"Mother!" Chelle clutched the large bath towel around her.

"Did you think they wouldn't look? They couldn't miss it." Charlotte still held her hand out.

Chelle reached back into the drawer and pulled out the beach towel she brought from home just in case she needed it. She opened the folds and extracted the offending bits of fabric. "Here. Take it. Can't you let me have any fun?"

Charlotte caught the bikini her daughter threw at her. "Fun? You call that fun? What happened to the daughter I raised to be a strong Christian girl?"

With defiant eyes, Chelle shouted, "Why does everything have to be about you? What about me?" She threw herself onto her bed and sobbed uncontrollably.

Charlotte stood, holding the still damp clothing while tears streamed down her own cheeks and her heart broke. *I lost it again. Why am I always doing that with Chelle?*

five

Chelle cried herself to sleep, and Charlotte paced the length of the cabin. This was not how she imagined spending this cruise with her daughter. Chelle seemed to be recovering from the loss of her father, but maybe she hurt more than she let on. Perhaps she hid it because she didn't want to add to her mother's pain.

I've got to do something to heal our hearts. Make tomorrow a new day. Our last day on an island. We need to build good memories together so when we get home, we'll have things to talk about. We have to reconnect.

Sure, Chelle was grieving, but Charlotte knew that her age worked against the situation. The mothers of Chelle's friends often talked about the battle of wills as young people pushed boundaries. That was what Chelle was doing, trying to find her boundaries. *I need wisdom in the morning.*

Charlotte stopped by the window. Tonight they had the drapes pulled back. Millions of stars twinkled in the sky like sparkling jewels against a velvet indigo background. A full moon made a bright path across the water, reaching from the horizon to the ship. Part of her wanted to step out and walk the magical, golden road to a new and better life. If only it could be that simple.

Well after midnight, Charlotte finally undressed and slipped between the clean sheets. Because they never left the stateroom after their excursions that day, the cabin stewards didn't have opportunity to come in and prepare the room for the night, leaving a whimsical animal made out of towels for their enjoyment. Charlotte didn't miss that as much as she missed the wonderful mint on her pillow. She was afraid she wouldn't get much sleep, but once she fell asleep, she didn't awaken until morning.

When Charlotte opened her eyes, Chelle sat on her own bed, with her knees drawn up, watching her mother. "Mom, I'm sorry. I knew I shouldn't do what I did, and I was mad that I'd gotten caught. Can you forgive me?"

Charlotte's heart melted. She went over to sit beside Chelle. "Of course. And you need to forgive me for losing my temper."

Chelle put her arms around her mother, and they shared a bear hug like the ones they used to share when she was younger.

"How about we do something together on Jamaica? It's our last chance on the cruise to go on an excursion together." Charlotte hoped she wasn't pushing too hard.

Chelle jumped up and got the cruise guidebook. "I want to do that waterfall thing everyone is talking about."

They pored over the list and chose the excursion that also included a visit to a working plantation and lunch on the beach.

"Let's hope there are still tickets available." Charlotte walked toward the phone. "We should have decided where we wanted to go that first day we spent at sea. If we had ordered our tickets then, we wouldn't have to worry about not getting some now."

When she called the purser, other passengers had turned in two tickets to that excursion, so Charlotte ordered them. They quickly dressed and went to the breakfast buffet at the Oceanic Grille. After finishing, they had to hurry to reach the theater in time for their excursion group to meet.

After an explanatory speech by one of the crewmembers, the group took the elevators down to deck two to exit the ship. Big white vans waited on the other side of the fence from the dock to whisk them away from Ocho Rios. Charlotte liked having her daughter with her on the bus.

Chelle eagerly took everything in. "There aren't as many palm trees here as on the other two islands and lots of other kinds of trees. Mom, why were Cozumel and Grand Cayman so flat, but Jamaica has mountains?"

"Jamaica was formed by volcanic action on the ocean floor, much like the Hawaiian Islands were. Cozumel and the Cayman Islands are coral islands that built up over time."

Chelle turned back from the window. "Oh yeah, we studied something about that kind of thing in science class. I had forgotten."

The people seated in front of them turned around and introduced themselves. The rest of the forty-five-minute drive to the plantation was spent getting acquainted.

After they exited the vans, Chelle turned all around, looking at everything. There was a lot to see, and Charlotte's heart gladdened because of her interest.

"Look at those funny tractor thingies."

"Those 'funny tractor thingies' are going to take us on a tour of the plantation." Charlotte led her daughter to the last vehicle to load passengers.

As they traveled through the lush tropical setting, their guide told them the history of the plantation, which had been producing tropical fruit since the eighteenth century. Sugar cane for both sugar and rum was another cash crop grown there. Finally, they reached a large packing shed with modern equipment and lots of workers.

"Look, Mom." Chelle pointed toward tables set up by a huge tree with branches spreading to provide a canopy of shade. "They have refreshments for us. I'm really thirsty."

Charlotte followed her. They drank punch and sampled sweet juicy pineapple, pieces of crunchy coconut, and chunks of fresh sugar cane, which they sucked on to get out the syrupy nectar.

"This punch is good." Chelle turned toward the Jamaican woman with the broad smile, who stood behind the table. "What's in it?"

"Oh, little bits o' this 'n' that. All the kinds of fruit grown on the plantation." Her musical accent floated through the humid air. "Would your mother like some punch with a little more punch?" Her eyebrows rose as she turned to Charlotte.

"No, thank you. This is just fine." Charlotte took another sip and reached for a large chunk of fresh coconut meat.

"Okay everybody." The guide stood in the center of the clearing holding a clipboard. "Come on now. We're going to the Great House."

After the short ride, they filed up on the wide, columned porch and through the double front doors. Charlotte loved the open feel of the rooms. Windows reached almost from the floor to the tall ceilings. They were wide open to let in the breeze, which was helped along by the many ceiling fans. Even so, she was glad she had worn her coolest gauzy culottes and tank top.

Furniture spread in pleasing arrangements in the large rooms told the history of the area. Pieces from the last three centuries blended together, giving the house a timeless feel. Charlotte was sure many of the antiques were valuable. If she owned this place, she wouldn't let tourists, who might damage something, troop through it.

"I'd love to live in a house like this, wouldn't you, Mom?"

Chelle's interest pleased Charlotte. "Sure, but only if we have servants to clean it. It's huge."

"But you could have some really great parties here."

Evidently the guide heard their conversation. "Oh, yes, there have been many wonderful parties in this house. Too bad the walls can't talk. What a history they would reveal. Celebrities from many countries have attended." He ended with a merry laugh.

Before Charlotte was ready to leave, he called them back to the vans for the ride to Dunn's River Falls. Chelle couldn't sit still; she was so excited for the chance to climb the giant waterway. Charlotte wasn't sure she even wanted to, but she did want to spend the whole day with Chelle.

On the beach, they were given rubber shoes to wear in the water. Charlotte glanced dubiously at the pair handed to her. "Are these clean?"

"Oh, yes, ma'am. We sanitize them each time between tours." The young Jamaican woman's teeth gleamed through her dark smile. "Can't have people passing anything bad around, now can we?"

They were divided into groups of ten. Charlotte was first in line for her group. After telling them to hold hands and not let go, the guide took Charlotte's hand and started up the rocks over which the water tumbled. This was no little waterfall. Several yards wide and taller than she could estimate, thousands of gallons of water a second had to be tumbling over the uneven formations. In some places, the water depth reached almost to her waist. She didn't feel confident as she stepped onto the uneven rocks. She wanted to be sure of her step each time.

Before long, the guide pulled on her wrist. "Come on, lady, you're too slow."

Charlotte felt like jerking her hand away from his, but he gripped her wrist too hard. "I want to be sure I have a safe place to put my foot."

"Just step in the place where I step. That's the safest spot." He wasn't smiling as most of the Jamaicans she'd seen before.

Charlotte looked at his feet. When he moved one of his, she put her foot in the same spot. She glanced up. They were still very near the bottom, and she couldn't see the top of the waterfall. This was going to be a long climb. With each movement, she followed the leader, but she wasn't enjoying all the effort it took to get up these cliffs covered with water. Hopefully, Chelle was. Finally, after what seemed like an eternity, they reached the top.

"Great. We made it." Charlotte tried to extricate her hand from the guide's.

"No, ma'am, we're not finished."

Charlotte looked at the large pool where they stood. Trees grew on both sides and shaded the lagoon.

When the last person on their team reached the plateau, the guide led them catty-corner across the gurgling water. On the other side, a waterfall about half as tall as the part they had already climbed rose above them.

Charlotte stopped, and Chelle plowed into her back. "Mom, what's wrong?"

"I don't want to climb up there. I'm really tired." She turned to the guide. "Is there no other way out of here?"

He gave a disgusted huff then pointed to the side. "See those steps leading out of the water?" She nodded. "You can go over there and walk up instead of climbing the waterfall."

Charlotte looked back at her daughter. "Would you be very disappointed if I did that?"

Chelle studied her mother's expression for a minute. "Not if you don't mind me climbing up the rest of the way without you."

When Charlotte read the understanding in her daughter's expression, she slogged through the water toward the wooden stairs.

❧

Gareth hadn't been able to get his thoughts off Charlotte and her daughter. He almost didn't hear Doug when he suggested that they take part in the Monopoly Tournament the next day.

"Why would we want to do that?"

"Sometimes you play some of the games. I just thought it would be good PR. Since this is a new ship. People like a captain who makes himself available to them, and word gets around."

"Okay, put us on the schedule."

Gareth didn't want to think about games. His mind was on other things. He had made sure the room steward took the invitation to dine at his table to the cabin and put it on Charlotte's pillow where she would be sure to find it. If she didn't come tonight, he would have to find a way to talk to her later. Something was wrong, but he couldn't figure out what. He didn't like this feeling of not being in control—of his own emotions as well as whatever was going on with Charlotte and her daughter. Maybe he had been at sea too long. Was it time to think about a position shoreside?

After arriving at the Captain's Cocktail Party, he took his usual non-alcoholic fruit punch and looked for Charlotte. When he didn't see her, he mingled with the guests, stopping to shake a hand here, compliment a lady there.

Usually, he didn't eat any of the hors d'oeuvres supplied by the chefs, but nervousness took him to the table. Of course, they were excellent, but before he realized how many he'd eaten while he was speaking to the various clusters of people, he started to feel a little full. Not a good move. With lobster and steak tonight at dinner, he wanted to save room.

The party seemed to take forever without Charlotte. He moved close to the door every time a new group arrived, but she didn't come. Finally, it was time to call everyone's attention and introduce the senior members of his staff, who were in their dress uniforms. When that task was completed, the orchestra struck up some swing dance music, and Gareth quietly slipped out with the rest of the crew. He didn't enjoy feeling like a teenager trying to catch a glimpse of his crush-of-the-week. This had to stop.

Everyone he invited to share his table at dinner arrived several minutes early, except the two Halloran women. The effort of trying to hide his disappointment nearly choked him. He leaned down to hear what the elderly woman sitting beside him was saying. Her extremely soft voice was almost drowned out, even though the dining room wasn't noisy.

"Captain—" A voice spoke over his shoulder. "I'm sorry we're late. It was my fault, not Mom's. She wanted to buy me a dress at the boutique, and I had a hard time choosing between this one and another one."

He quickly stood and pulled out the chairs for both Charlotte and Chelle. The lightness of his heart made him feel that he could take off flying. "You're not too late." He pushed in the teenager's chair and reached for Charlotte's. The delicate fragrance of her perfume filled his senses making him feel almost intoxicated. "That dress was a very good choice. Besides, we haven't started ordering yet."

%

Charlotte perused the extensive menu, not able to make up her mind. Seafood, prime rib, other steaks. Even though her stomach growled at the thought of the food, she couldn't decide.

"What will you be having, Charlotte?" Gareth's deep baritone voice settled into her spirit.

"I can't make up my mind." She read the entrees once again. "I love both lobster and prime rib."

Gareth signaled the waiter, who hurried over. "Mrs Halloran will have both the lobster and the prime rib."

Charlotte gasped. "I won't be able to eat all that."

"That's okay. You can try as many items as you want to, and you don't have to eat it all."

Charlotte swallowed the words that bubbled to get out. Words about waste and people going hungry. She'd heard them often enough when she was growing up, and she'd even used them on Chelle plenty of times.

Chelle leaned to look around her mother. "Does that mean that I can order more than one dessert, Captain?" The twinkle in her eyes told Charlotte that she was almost joking, but not quite.

"And"—Gareth held up his hand to the waiter—"when we get the dessert menu, Miss Halloran won't need one. Just bring her one of each."

The waiter didn't bat an eye. He gave Gareth a slight bow and moved on to the next person.

"You didn't really mean that, did you, Captain?" Chelle's eyes widened as she looked at him and one eyebrow rose quizzically.

"I most certainly did."

Laughter echoed around the table as the other people decided to order extra items, too.

After dinner, Charlotte and Chelle went into the Centrum to have their formal portrait made in front of a painting of the ship at night.

"Maybe we should have done this before dinner." Charlotte put Chelle in front and turned them both to the side. "I probably weighed less then."

A deep chuckle drifted down toward them. Charlotte glanced up to see Gareth give her a wink before he headed toward the ballroom where the cocktail party for the first seating should be in full swing. When the photographer told them to smile, Charlotte knew she had beaten him to it. The tall captain gave her something special to smile about.

After the photographer finished taking a couple of pictures of them together, then one of each of them alone, they moved out of the way for the next group.

"What do you want to do now?" Charlotte asked her daughter.

"We didn't go to the other midnight buffet when we were on the way to Cozumel." Chelle took her mother's arm and pulled her toward the elevator. "Let's go to the one tonight."

"I can't believe you'll want to eat again." Charlotte rubbed her full stomach. Thankfully, this dress wasn't a sheath. She'd be popping out of it after that dinner.

The bell on the elevator dinged, and the doors opened, spilling out a group dressed in a variety of ways. Some had gone to the formal dinner while others evidently spent their time near the pools or in the casino.

Only the two of them boarded the car, and Chelle punched the button for their deck. "We don't have to eat anything.

I just want to see it. I heard people talking about ice sculptures and fancy foods at the captain's midnight buffet. But I'm not wearing this dress or these shoes any longer."

"We need to look nice, though." Charlotte tried to decide what to put on.

The elevator stopped and opened. "I brought a sundress that I wear to church." Chelle led the way down the hall. "It should be all right for tonight."

six

On Friday morning, Charlotte planned to sleep in, but Chelle woke early. Since boarding the cruise ship, sleeping late wasn't in her vocabulary.

"We have to experience everything on board." Chelle pulled on a navy knit top with her navy, red, and white shorts, then fluffed out her hair. "We might not ever do another cruise."

Charlotte decided to go along with her teenager as long as Chelle was in the mood to spend time together. She was sure that her daughter would find things to do without her later in the day. "What did you have in mind?"

Chelle sat on the side of Charlotte's bed while she put on her sneakers. "There's a Monopoly tournament this morning. I think we could win."

"You and your dad could've won. I never was as good a player as either of you." Charlotte scooted around her daughter to stand up and stretch. "But if you want me for your partner, I'm game. What time does it start?"

"Nine o'clock, in the Dancing Waves Ballroom. I think it's on deck five at the back of the ship."

They rushed through their breakfast and barely made it to the large round room in time to take their place at a table. Charlotte wondered how long this tournament would last. She could see it going through lunch and maybe even dinner, if everyone played the way she did.

The activities director stood in the glow cast by a spotlight, holding a microphone. "There's a one-hour limit to each round. We'll tally the money, property value, houses, and hotels. The team with the highest dollar amount wins and moves on to the next round."

Okay, that'll keep it from lasting all day. Charlotte counted the tables. With only sixteen people around four tables, the tournament would be three rounds. Gareth sat on the opposite side of the table at the far end. Surely he wasn't going to play.

"We are privileged"—the activities director gestured with a flourish—"to have our captain and the purser taking part in the tournament." Applause filled the room. "I will warn you, though, that these men play a very good game. You'll have to be an expert to beat them."

According to the chatter going on around the room, several passengers felt up to the task. Charlotte glanced back toward Gareth, and her gaze collided with his. The twinkle in his eyes tugged at her heart making her want him to win. But Chelle wouldn't like that. Now she felt torn.

"Okay, people." The activities director drew everyone's attention. "There is a prize of a one hundred dollar shipboard gift certificate. You can purchase more photographs or spend it in any of our onboard stores, or even use it to reduce your account."

Hoots and shouts of items different participants wanted included booze and the casino. Charlotte hoped someone else besides those people would win the prize.

When the bell dinged to start the game, her table began playing in earnest. However, there was plenty of time to get acquainted with the couple from New Orleans who made up the other team.

"Have you been on any other cruises?" Charlotte's question broke the ice.

They quickly answered before arranging their money in

neat piles beside the board. The older married couple soon proved to be just as intent on the game as Chelle. Between her turns to play, Charlotte looked around the room. Just as everywhere else she had been on the ship, the ballroom boasted the finest accoutrements. On the carpet in shades of soft teals and burgundies, plush seats ringed the marble dance floor. The brass rails and other fittings sparkled in the bright sunlight that streamed through the windows across the back of the ship.

By the end of the hour, both teams at their table had amassed quite a lot of money and property. Activity crew-members went to each table to tabulate. Only five dollars separated the two teams, with Charlotte and Chelle on top. Their competitors assured them that they hoped she and Chelle would win the tournament.

In round two, the Halloran women played a fun-loving team, joking their way through the game. Charlotte remembered the two out-of-shape, suntanned men as some of the most vocal about the booze and gambling, so she really wanted to beat them. All her concentration went into the game. Once again, she and Chelle came out on top by a small margin. Their competitors wished them luck before they left to find some liquid refreshment other than the iced tea and water available to the players. At least the couple who'd lost the first round to them waited to see who prevailed in the tournament. Charlotte enjoyed having them as a cheering section.

With all the tables removed, except the one for the final round, Charlotte and Chelle chose their seats. Charlotte looked around to see who won from the other table. After she and Chelle sat in chairs opposite each other, Gareth and his purser slid into the other two. Charlotte glanced up and noticed a twinkle in Gareth's eyes. *This round should prove interesting.*

ta

Gareth had suspected, when they sat down at the first table, that he and Doug would be in the last game. He had hoped that wouldn't happen, until he noticed Charlotte and Chelle. That made him want to win the first two rounds, and he wanted their opponents in the last one to be the charming Hallorans. The other players at their tables in the first two rounds didn't really know very much about Monopoly. They just wanted to have fun, so it was easy for Doug and him to be victorious.

He took a moment before they sat at the final round table to tell Doug what he planned to do. He hoped he could be subtle enough for the women not to realize his strategy. Charlotte and Chelle must win the tournament. In the past when he took part in activities like this, if he won, a drawing among all the contestants was held to choose who would receive the gift certificate. The women might not win in a drawing, so they had to win the game.

Gareth knew that Charlotte had been having trouble with her teen, so he wanted Chelle to be happy with something they did together. Perhaps the rest of the cruise would go more smoothly for them and help make a connection that couldn't be broken.

He smiled at each of the women. "May the better team win."

Chelle took up the challenge. "And we're that best team, aren't we, Mom?"

Charlotte nodded as she smiled at him. He liked the twinkle in her eyes.

It didn't take long to see who the strongest player on the other team was. He knew it might not be right to pray for the dice to fall in the women's favor, but he did it anyway. At least it wasn't for selfish gain.

About half an hour into the game, Chelle hit the table with her open hand. Thankfully, it didn't disturb the items on the board. "Captain and Mr. Baxter, I see what you're doing."

Gareth tried to sound nonchalant. "We're trying to win this game." Doug nodded his agreement.

The teenager leaned forward and looked first at Doug, then at him. "I thought you were, but some of the things you've done in the game weren't smart, and I know that both of you are very smart. Besides, you've already won two games."

"Our competitors weren't very good players." Doug glanced at him as if it was now his turn to say something.

Gareth looked Chelle straight in the eyes. "You're just too good for us." He tried not to laugh at her serious expression.

"That's just the point."

Gareth noticed that Charlotte watched her daughter with admiration. He agreed with her assessment.

"I'm a very good player." Chelle's voice sounded like hardened steel. "And you're not letting me show you. I want to win on my own merits or not at all."

Gareth had underestimated the girl, and she deserved his best. He nodded to Doug and read agreement in his friend's eyes. "Okay, no holds barred. We're going to show you just how well we play."

"Fine." Chelle gave the dice to Doug. "It's your turn."

The rest of the game intensified. Gareth realized that both teams were evenly matched. He decided that the girl could play better than her mother could, but Charlotte was no slouch at the game. Every move had to be carefully considered. When the timekeeper rang his bell, Gareth was sure he and Doug had won. He just hoped that the drawing would make the two women winners of the gift certificate.

When the activities director finished adding up the money, property, houses, and hotels, Chelle and Charlotte won by ten dollars.

The teenager jumped up, and her fist shot into the air high above her head. "All right!"

❧

"Mom, we won." Charlotte caught her daughter as she launched herself into her mother's outstretched arms. "We beat the captain and Mr. Baxter." Chelle danced around pulling Charlotte with her.

"Yes, we did." Charlotte took a quick breath when they stopped moving. "I'm proud of you."

"Okay, ladies." The activities director spoke into the microphone. "Come up here and collect your prize."

Those other participants who still remained in the ballroom gave a rousing cheer. Chelle pulled her mother to the front of the room with her then took a bow. Charlotte knew her daughter was enjoying this very much.

"Give it to Chelle." Charlotte smiled at the director. "She's really the one who earned it."

The man placed the envelope in Chelle's hand then made an announcement about the afternoon activities.

"Mom." Chelle folded the envelope and pushed it into the pocket of her shorts. "I want to eat lunch up on the Oceanic Deck with some of the other girls I've met. We'll probably spend quite a bit of the afternoon up there. Is that okay?"

Charlotte nodded, and her daughter hurried away. Everyone else had streamed from the room after the announcements were over. Everyone except Gareth.

"I'm not needed on the bridge for a while, Charlotte." She couldn't keep her interest from sparking at the captain's words.

He didn't leave her in suspense for long. "Perhaps we could spend some of the day together." When she nodded, he took her arm and led her toward the front of the ship. "I want to show you one of my favorite places on the *Pearl of the Ocean*."

They walked the length of deck five, passing through the photo gallery.

"Let's stop and see what pictures are up now." Charlotte tugged on Gareth's arm.

After the second day, she hadn't been looking to see what pictures were there, waiting to check for more interesting ones later. The photographers took a lot of pictures of everyone on the cruise. In addition to the fun pictures from the first day, there were shots of her as she disembarked at each island. In the first two, she was alone, but on Jamaica, the picture with Chelle was a playful pose. She would buy that later.

"Here's one with you sitting beside me at dinner." Gareth's deep voice sent shivers through Charlotte.

She stared at the candid shot of them on the night of the Captain's Gala. With his blond good looks and her dark hair, the photo drew her attention. Did they really look like that? Almost as if they belonged together? She decided right then to buy that one when he wasn't with her.

"I like this formal portrait of you and Chelle." He pointed toward the eight by ten.

Charlotte would definitely buy that one, too. She could see her balance on her account mounting.

"Maybe you should have kept the gift certificate for yourself."

She wondered if he had read her mind. "It's okay. I budgeted enough to be able to spend for some fun things on the trip. I'm even planning to see if Chelle would want to do the spa tomorrow with me."

When they reached the smaller elevator bank near the front of the ship, Gareth held the door open for her to enter. He pushed the button for deck eleven. If Charlotte remembered the map correctly, the short deck only covered the very front of deck ten.

They stepped off into a tiered room with tables and chairs on each riser, as well as a large flat area on the highest level, and windows all around. Charlotte turned completely to take in the whole panorama. The Gulf of Mexico spread around them as far as the eye could see. The only things besides water were smudges on the horizon, too far away to tell what they were.

"Are those other ships?" She turned to look up at Gareth and caught her breath.

He was standing very close, and he wasn't looking at the view. The intensity of his gaze sent heat coursing through her. She turned quickly back toward the windows. This couldn't be happening to her. She would just have to be sure she didn't get so close to him. Although a shipboard romance sounded like fun, she had never been a person for light flirtations. Anything other than friendship would be too intense. But there wasn't any reason they couldn't be just friends.

"That one"—Gareth pointed toward the right—"is another cruise ship coming this direction. You'll be able to see it better soon." He motioned toward another smudge. "That is an offshore oil rig."

"Way out here?"

"Yes, there are a number of them in the Gulf." Gareth raised a hand and traced the outline of her cheek with gentle fingers.

Charlotte stepped away from his magnetic presence. "What's this room called?"

Gareth dropped his hand to his side and glanced around the room then back at her. "This is the Oyster Shell. At night it's a bar, but in the daytime, it makes a good observation deck. I come here often when I'm not on duty."

"I can see why."

❧

Gareth gazed at the water. The startled look in Charlotte's eyes danced between him and the waves. Why had he done that? He'd frightened her. If they had given in to the urge to share a kiss in the solitude up here, it would have taken their relationship to a whole new level. Evidently Charlotte wasn't ready for that. Was he?

Of course not.

"Let's go down to deck nine and have lunch." He stepped over to the elevator door. "The theme is Tex-Mex in the Oceanic Grill today. Do you like that kind of food?" What a lame question!

"It's one of my favorites. Remember, I'm from Texas." Her smile speared straight to his heart. "I just hope your chefs know how to prepare it properly."

He laughed at her audacity. "I think you'll be pleasantly surprised."

When they stepped off of the elevator, the long lunch line had dwindled, so they walked through and made their choices. Gareth chose a table that wasn't near any other people. There would be interruptions, but maybe not too many.

After a pleasant lunch, they went back down to deck five. This time they walked through the hallway that divided the shops.

"Today there's a fine jewelry sale in this store." He pointed toward one gift shop. "Would you like to check anything out?"

Charlotte led the way toward the glass cases containing a

myriad of colored and clear stones set in a variety of styles. Her eyes lit up when she saw the display of amethyst pieces.

"I've always loved colored gemstones." She moved down the side of the case.

"Would you like to see anything up close?" Gareth smiled at the cruise line employee who asked the question. "I'll be glad to let you try some of these items on."

He wondered who bought Charlotte jewelry since her husband was gone. Maybe she didn't get new items. He watched her try on several. She kept going back to one set with drop earrings and another drop on a slender gold chain. Finally, she took them off and moved farther down, looking at other items. Gareth took a piece of paper out of his pocket and jotted a note on it. He folded it and thrust it into an employee's hand, telling her to give it to the person waiting on Charlotte.

Maybe he was crazy. He wasn't looking for a permanent relationship, but he knew that he didn't want what was happening between him and Charlotte to end when she stepped off the ship in New Orleans. Somehow, he was going to find a way for it to continue, and someday he would give her those amethyst pieces.

seven

"Mom!"

The voice called to Charlotte through the veil of a pleasant dream, tugging her to a state of being half-awake. "What?" She didn't want to open her eyes yet.

Chelle flopped down on the side of Charlotte's bed and shook her. Charlotte forced her eyelids apart and stared at her daughter with what she hoped was a questioning expression.

"It's our last day on the cruise. We need to make the most of it." Chelle leaned over to fasten her sandals.

Charlotte scooted up in the bed and leaned her pillow against the wall behind her. Chelle went to the window, pulled the heavy drapes open, and pushed the sheers to one side.

"See what a beautiful day it is."

Charlotte rubbed her eyes and glanced at her watch, which she had forgotten to remove when she went to bed last night. "Nine o'clock! No wonder I'm hungry." She scrambled out of bed and padded over to the desk, where she took off the watch and set it by her purse. "I'll take a quick shower, and we can go to breakfast at the Oceanic Grill. It's on the same deck as the spa." She turned to her daughter. "I made appointments for both of us to get massages, then spa manicures and pedicures."

Chelle smiled. "For me, too?"

"I thought it would be fun."

After her quick shower, Charlotte twisted her hair up in back and anchored it with a large clip. Maybe she would have time to shampoo it later today. "I don't think we'll want to eat very much before the massage."

×

When they walked across the atrium section of deck nine, the warm air felt humid, probably due to the sparkling blue swimming pool in the middle and the freestanding gazebo-type structures near each corner that housed whirlpools. Many passengers already filled the water amenities, enjoying their therapeutic benefits. Thankfully, the spa was air-conditioned.

"Welcome." A young woman in a cruise uniform greeted them as the door opened. "Are you Charlotte and Chelle Halloran?"

Chelle hurried across the room to the desk. "Yes, I'm Chelle."

"Do you want to have your massages in the same room?" The women held a pen poised above the appointment book.

Charlotte turned to Chelle, wanting her to make the decision. "Sure."

"Do you have a preference as to whether a man or woman gives you the massage?"

A startled look flitted across Chelle's face. "No, whoever is really good works for me."

Her insight surprised Charlotte.

When they had removed most of their clothing and climbed up on their own table to lie on their stomachs, another young woman came in and covered each of them with a sheet. "Carlos will do one massage, and Jeanie will do the other. Does it matter which?"

Chelle quickly answered, "I want Jeanie."

It didn't matter to Charlotte, but she was glad that Chelle hadn't asked for the man.

Soft music wafted through the air, mingling with the

tropical scent from the candles that sat on a ledge along two walls of the room. Charlotte began to relax. So far this cruise had turned out to be an emotional roller-coaster ride, and she needed something to soothe her.

Carlos pulled the sheet to her waist and anointed her with scented oil that mixed well with the fresh perfume from the candles. As he rubbed it into her skin, his fingers found all the stress knots and gently, but firmly, worked them out.

"Mom, could you believe what that man in the show did last night?" Evidently Chelle wanted to talk.

"Are you over your embarrassment yet?" Charlotte chuckled as she turned her head to look at her daughter.

"It doesn't seem so bad this morning, but when he took me up on stage and sang to me, I couldn't believe that so many people were looking at me." Chelle's voice slowed, probably from the effects of the massage. "I don't mind being in front of a group, if there are people I know. But that theater holds a bunch of people, and I didn't know many of them. It might be good practice for when I go to college, though."

Charlotte laughed. "You do have another year before that."

❧

Because of their light breakfast, Chelle and Charlotte went down to the dining room for lunch right after their time at the spa. They barely made it before the dining room closed.

While they were waiting for their lunch to arrive, Chelle held up her hands. "I like this color on my nails."

Charlotte chuckled. "My pale pink is more to my liking than that electric blue on yours. I can't believe you also had it put on your toenails. You don't really have anything to wear with it."

"M–o–m, your nails don't have to match your clothes anymore."

After they finished most of their food, Chelle asked her mother if she could try to find some of her new friends she'd met on the ship. Charlotte waved her away and sipped more of the wonderful coffee. She knew they served Starbucks at the Ben & Jerry's Ice Cream shop on deck six, but she hadn't realized that they also had it here.

When she left the dining room, she went up to check out deck eight. On one side of the Centrum, a computer room allowed passengers to go online. . .for a price. She hadn't wanted to read e-mail. This vacation meant getting away from all that. Besides, she really wasn't that comfortable with the new electronic world. All but one of the eight computers had passengers sitting in front of them. Evidently not everyone shared Charlotte's feelings.

The library on deck seven sounded like a good idea. Of course, she hadn't had time to read the book she borrowed off the shelves, so she didn't want to return it, but she took the elevator to that level anyway. She walked to the wall of windows and stared out at the gently undulating waves. Tiny white caps indicated that there was a wind, but the movement of the ship was so slight, she couldn't feel it unless she concentrated. Off in the distance, another cruise ship moved toward them. Probably on the way to the Caribbean. They should pass each other before long. Farther away, two more oil rig platforms were silhouetted against the bright blue sky.

"Charlotte."

The familiar voice called to something inside her. She placed a hand on her stomach to calm the butterflies and turned. "Gareth. Are you on a break again?"

"Yes. The ship almost runs itself when we're at sea. You know, with satellite positioning and computers, all we have to do is keep watch on the equipment. This is Homer's afternoon on duty." His long legs quickly brought him across the carpeted floor.

❧

Even with her hair bunched up under that plastic clamp thing, Charlotte took Gareth's breath away. Black curls had escaped and framed her face, making her skin look fresh and her blue eyes sparkle. He wanted to pull her into his arms and kiss her until she, too, was breathless. How could he feel such a strong attraction when he vowed never to get involved with another woman?

Almost of its own volition, his hand reached up and twirled one of the curls around his finger. At the first touch, Charlotte held her breath, but she didn't pull away. The expression in her eyes was wary, but inviting. He had to break this magnetism. He dropped his hand to his side and looked down at the couch.

"Let's sit here and talk." The words sounded husky even to his own ears.

"Okay." Charlotte sat on the far end.

He followed her, but instead of sitting by the other end, he chose the middle, closer to her. After placing his arm along the back of the sofa, he glanced into her eyes. "So what did you do this morning?" Maybe that question could move them to safer ground.

Charlotte held up her hands. "Chelle and I had a massage, then a spa manicure and pedicure."

He wanted to take them in his and kiss the fingertips. "They look nice."

"Just nice?" Charlotte laughed, the sound music to his ears. "Nice is such an insipid word."

"Okay." He took a moment to compose his answer. "Your

hand is lovelier than any other hand on the whole ship. How was that?"

This time, he joined in her laughter. As they continued to talk, Charlotte's gaze often glanced toward the waves outside the windows. She seemed to sink lower into the cushions of the sofa, and her eyes started drifting closed. He knew how relaxing a massage could be. Maybe she needed a nap. When her eyes finally stayed shut, her head began to loll. Gareth slipped his arm around her shoulders and pulled her toward him, so she leaned against his chest. She must have felt comfortable, because she snuggled closer without waking.

She looked so beautiful sleeping—younger and, well, relaxed. He felt free to gaze at her as much as he wanted. A slight sound from the door drew his attention. Chelle stared into his eyes. Her frown turned into a stricken expression. Before he could react, she turned and ran away.

Gareth gazed down at Charlotte's head nestled against his chest. Should he tell her what happened? Would it help or drive more of a wedge between mother and daughter?

❧

During dinner, Gareth tried not to pay any more attention to Charlotte than he did any other woman at his table. Even though the bright freshness of her face had the same pull as the North Star on a compass, he intentionally looked at the other women, especially Chelle. From the first moment they arrived, the teenager's expression told him that she was watching him. So he had included her in every conversation, asking her opinion on several of the subjects discussed. During the course of the meal, she seemed to relax, so he probably had been right not to worry her mother about Chelle seeing them in the library.

Charlotte pushed her dessert plate away and moved the

napkin from her lap to the table. "I can't take another bite. . . even though I love crème brûlée."

Chelle followed her mother's example then moved her chair away from the table. "Mom, I want to meet some of my friends up on deck. Okay?"

After studying her daughter's face, Charlotte nodded. "Okay. Just don't stay out very late."

It didn't take Chelle long to weave a path around the tables and exit through the open doorway. She glanced back for only a moment before she was completely out of the room. Gareth felt her stare as if it were a physical punch. Maybe she hadn't gotten over her problem with what happened earlier.

The teenager proved to be the catalyst to start a mass exit from the table. In a couple of minutes, only he and Charlotte remained.

"Would you like to take a walk on deck?" Gareth pulled her chair out and offered her his arm.

Charlotte smiled up at him, slid her hand through the crook of his elbow, and placed it on his forearm. He felt the touch through the uniform jacket and the shirt he wore underneath. Other people milled around on the outside deck of level four where the dining room was, so he led the way to the elevator. They walked down the hallways on deck eight to reach the bridge. He ushered her through to the small balcony on the side.

"Am I supposed to be here?" Charlotte's skin, bathed in the bright moonlight, took on the delicate shine of a rare pearl.

He wanted to touch her cheek, but instead he leaned his arms on the railing and faced the wind, which was enhanced by the forward movement of the ship. "It's all right if I bring you." He turned and leaned back against the rail so he could watch her expression.

"I never get tired of looking at the moon reflected on the water." Her eyes traced a track along the light path then turned toward the heavens. "And the stars are brighter out here over the water. It's so beautiful." Her last word was a whisper.

And you're so beautiful, Charlotte. Did he dare say it aloud, or would the intimacy of the isolated place lead them down a road they weren't ready to travel? Charlotte rubbed her hands on her bare upper arms.

"Is it too cool out here for you?" He pulled her close and held her against his chest, tempted to kiss her, but not succumbing to the temptation. "We could go to my quarters and talk. Homer and Marilyn will be nearby."

Gareth felt Charlotte's head nod before she whispered, "Okay."

When he slid his key card into the door, Marilyn stuck her head out of their quarters. "I have a pot of coffee made. Would you two like some?"

⋅☙⋅

The Wilsons only stayed and visited a few minutes, and Charlotte was glad they left both Gareth's door and the door to their apartment open. Gareth moved from his chair across the room to sit near her on the sofa. She slipped off her shoes, which weren't very comfortable, and pulled her feet up beside her, spreading her full skirt to cover them.

"Tonight is the last night of the cruise." She tried to keep the wistful note out of her tone.

"I know." Gareth leaned forward and held his hands loosely between his knees. "I've been thinking about it ever since we left the library."

"I can't believe I fell asleep up there." She ran her fingers through her hair pushing the curls away from her face.

"It was probably because of the massage. Have you had one

before?" Gareth leaned back and rested his arms along the back of the plush leather sofa.

She shook her head. "No, it was my first."

"You may have been tired from all the activities, too." When he smiled, the skin beside his eyes crinkled.

This man would be the perfect one to have a shipboard romance with. . .if he weren't the captain. . .and if she were ready for such a thing. "I've really enjoyed the cruise, especially the time I've spent with you."

"Charlotte, tell me about your husband."

His question startled her. What could she tell him about Philip? "He was in the military when we got married. A helicopter pilot. Chelle was a baby when he was sent to the Middle East. Philip made medical evacuations and was used in rescue operations. I worried about him all the time, but he came through that without a scratch." She glanced at Gareth and noticed his rapt attention to what she was saying. "He went to the police academy when he got out of the service. He loved helping people. Many of the officers had second jobs to supplement their incomes. Philip sold insurance, again because he believed it helped people." Her leg started tingling as if it was going to sleep, so she thrust one foot out in front of her and tapped it on the floor. "He had never had even a close encounter with disaster until that night a year ago." She stopped to swallow the lump in her throat.

Gareth's hand covered hers. "You don't have to go on, if you don't want to."

"It's okay." She turned over the hand under his until their palms were facing, interlacing her fingers with his. "I couldn't believe that he had been in such dangerous professions, but he was killed on the safe job."

Gareth shifted closer. "Selling insurance?"

Charlotte laughed. "No. He was coming home from the insurance office after staying until two in the morning doing paperwork. He stopped to help a stranded motorist on the freeway, and a drunk driver hit and killed him."

He pulled his hand free and gently gathered her into his arms. "I'm sorry. We've both had to face hard times."

She nodded against his comforting chest. "I know. That's why I don't want to become too close to anyone again. It hurts too much to lose them." But she was very close to Gareth right now, and it felt good.

❧

Gareth felt the moment her stiffness relaxed, and he tightened his embrace. "I know. Losing Britte was too hard." His breath stirred her dark curls, tickling his cheek, but he didn't try to move away.

Finally, he sat back and lifted his head. "You do know that something is happening between us, don't you?"

Charlotte pulled away and leaned down, slowly working her high-heeled sandals onto her feet. "It can't be. That part of my life is over. . . . Never. . ." Her voice drifted off into nothingness.

"Maybe I should go back to my cabin." She looked at her wristwatch. "It's getting pretty late. It's not really fair to give Chelle a curfew and then get to the cabin so much later myself."

Gareth stood then pulled her to her feet. "Okay." He turned her to face him and kept his hands on her shoulders. "I'm not sorry for what is happening." He kissed the end of her pert nose. "I'm not going to push you for more than you can give, but I want a relationship with you, even if it's only as a friend."

She let out a relieved sigh. "Yes, I want us to be friends."

Gareth wasn't going to let her go to her cabin alone. He

didn't care what anyone else thought. He would escort her to her door.

They strolled down the hallway and took the elevator to deck three. Then they walked two-thirds of the way along the length of that hallway, making small talk as they went.

"I want to be quiet, so I don't wake Chelle," Charlotte whispered as she slipped her key card in and out of the slot. She pushed the handle down and the door swept open.

Gareth glanced into the stateroom. All the lights were on, but no one was there. "Do you want me to make sure everything is all right?"

"She's probably just in the bathroom." Charlotte tapped on the closed door.

Nothing.

"Chelle, are you in there?" Charlotte paused then opened the door.

The bathroom was empty.

Fear shot through Charlotte's expression and settled into her eyes. "Where can she be?"

Gareth had to stop himself from laughing. "She has to be on the ship. We're a long way from land."

She turned toward him and took hold of his lapels. "Gareth, I told her to not stay out late. By now, the only thing going on is gambling or night clubbing, right?"

"Or she could be up on the pool deck."

"We have to find her." Charlotte wasn't far from hysteria as she rushed out the door.

eight

Gareth quickly closed the door to the cabin and caught up with Charlotte before she reached the lobby that contained the closest bank of elevators. He took her by the shoulders. "You need to calm down. You don't want to get Chelle, or anyone else, upset." He crushed her against his chest and rubbed her back. "It's going to be okay. She's probably trying to assert her independence. Isn't that what teenagers do?"

Charlotte sobbed once then pulled back. "You're right. I just can't lose her, too."

He leaned down until his face was even with hers. "You are not going to lose her tonight." Charlotte was so upset, he decided it would better to get crewmembers to search for Chelle.

After he guided her to the elevator, he punched the button for deck five. They exited the car, and he hurried Charlotte around the Centrum to the Purser's office. Two staff members manned the front desk, but he didn't stop to talk to them. He pulled Charlotte around the tall counter and through the doorway behind it. When he reached Doug's office, he stuck his head in. One of the assistant pursers was on duty.

"Do you know where Doug is?"

The young woman didn't bat an eye, even though he couldn't ever remember being in this area of the ship when she was on duty. "He said he planned to watch a movie tonight."

When they reached the purser's quarters, Gareth knocked

on the door. "Doug, are you decent? I have someone with me."

"Be there in a minute." Gareth could barely hear the answer through the well-insulated wall.

Doug finally opened the door while still tucking in his T-shirt. He scanned Gareth's face, then looked beyond him to Charlotte and pulled the door open wider. "Come in. I had to pick up a little of the clutter before I opened the door."

Gareth was sure he had. His friend wasn't a slob, but he also wasn't Mister Neatnik. "We have a little problem. Can we sit down and talk about it?" Hoping the relaxed atmosphere would calm some of Charlotte's fears, he guided her to the sofa.

"Can I offer you something to drink?" Doug asked while he clicked off the TV.

"No." Charlotte's word was a whisper. She cleared her throat. "No, thank you."

Doug took a seat on his bed and glanced from one of them to the other. "What's the problem?"

Gareth answered before Charlotte could. He hoped he could keep everything calmer that way. "Charlotte's daughter should be in her room, but she isn't. Can you get two or three of your best people, who can search for her without causing a stir, and send them out?"

"Sure." Doug went to his desk and pulled a notebook toward him. He picked up his phone and punched three buttons. "Tell Manuel, Aretha, and Reuben that I want to see them. . . ." He turned toward Gareth and covered the mouthpiece. "In your quarters?" When Gareth nodded, he told the person on the other end of the line.

Gareth took Charlotte's hand in his. "They will be discreet. Let's go up to the apartment and wait for them."

After they stood, Gareth held his hand out to Doug. "Thank you."

"I'm coming right behind you." His friend reached for his uniform shirt and thrust his arms in.

❧

Charlotte felt as though she were in a daze while Gareth led her to his quarters. She didn't notice anything about the parts of the ship they passed.

When they arrived, Marilyn stood in the doorway of her husband's apartment. "Is there anything I can do? Maybe bring something to eat or drink?"

Charlotte looked at Gareth, and he nodded. "That would be nice."

Marilyn brought a tray over almost before Charlotte was settled on the couch. Doug came in behind her, followed by three other crewmembers. He quickly crossed the room and perched on the edge of the sofa beside Charlotte.

"Do you have a picture of your daughter we can show our people? Or should we look in the photo shop?"

"I think I have one here." Charlotte pulled the chain handle of her small purse from her shoulder. She had almost forgotten it was there. She rummaged in her wallet until she found Chelle's school picture. That was the only one she had. She handed it to the purser.

Doug stood and gave it to one of the people waiting by the door. "Each of you should look closely at this. Memorize the girl's features, then search the ship. Spread out and don't miss a single place that's open to passengers." He looked at the one female in the group. "Aretha, you take another woman you can trust with you, and check every women's restroom and dressing room on the ship. One of you can stay outside the door and watch the corridors while the other one goes in.

That way if she walks by, you won't miss her."

He turned toward Charlotte. "Can they take this picture with them?"

Charlotte nodded. "Shouldn't I go, too?"

Gareth placed a hand on her shoulder. "We need to keep you in one place, so whoever finds her will know where to bring her."

When the crewmembers left, the purser went with them.

Marilyn set the tray on the table in front of the couch. "Here's coffee, iced tea, cookies, even ice water. What can I get for you?"

Charlotte knew that if she ate anything, it would catch on the lump in her throat. "I am thirsty. Maybe some water."

Marilyn put ice cubes into a tall goblet. They tinkled against the glass, making tiny musical sounds. Charlotte recognized that the container must be crystal. *What funny things you think about when you're trying not to be upset.*

After she gave the glass to Charlotte, Marilyn turned to Gareth. "Do you want me to stay here, or should I get a cabin steward for you?"

Gareth looked down at Charlotte. "Which would you prefer?" How like him to be so caring.

"I'd appreciate Marilyn's company. . .if she wants to stay."

"Okay, I'll join the search."

In one way, Charlotte was glad, but in another, she wished he would stay with her. She didn't really know what she wanted. . . except for Chelle to be all right. What if she fell overboard? If she were with other teenagers and they did something stupid, it could happen. They might be afraid of getting into trouble, and maybe they wouldn't have told anyone. . . . All these wild thoughts were making her crazy.

Marilyn sat beside her on the couch. She patted Charlotte's

clasped hands. "I know you're probably imagining all kinds of things that could've happened to your daughter. Don't. Let's not think about the bad things. Let's believe that God is taking care of her, and she'll be with us very soon. Can I pray with you?"

Charlotte agreed. Why hadn't she thought about praying? Because she hadn't really turned to God for anything since He let Philip die. She had attended church, but she was just going through the motions because she wanted Chelle to be involved. Was God trying to get her attention? *Oh God, please don't take Chelle away from me, too.*

⁂

When Gareth arrived in Doug's office, the search party was dividing the ship into sectors for each of them to cover. Gareth and Doug took decks nine, ten, and eleven. They went in opposite directions when they stepped off the elevator near the front of deck nine. That way, they could cover twice as much area. Gareth walked through the Oceanic Grille, even though it had been closed for hours. The band playing in front of the bar near the outside pool almost deafened him. The people who liked to party late into the night were also the ones who made the most noise. He met Doug in front of the solarium.

"So you didn't find her in the pools or whirlpools?"

Doug shook his head. "You know they're reserved for adults."

"I have a feeling this teenager thinks she is an adult."

They quickly climbed the stairs that led to the jogging track that ringed deck ten. Instead of going different ways, they walked together this time. Gareth almost expected to see the girl trying to rappel on the climbing wall. He remembered Charlotte saying she had told her not to try it. But thankfully, she wasn't back there, especially since no crewmember would be there to help her at this time of night.

After rounding the prow of deck ten, the two men climbed the stairs that led to the Oyster Shell. When the glass doors slid open, loud voices interspersed with equally loud disco music poured out and surrounded the men as they entered the room. Gareth didn't like to come up here at night. He never had been one to go to nightclubs, even before he became a Christian.

A constant pulse of variegated strobe lights bathed the dance floor and nearby tables of the dimly lit room. Gyrating bodies crowded the hardwood floor under a rotating mirror ball. Gareth scanned the room, looking especially at the face of every female with long dark curls. *There she is. . . . Her mother won't be happy to see her.*

Chelle wore a much too sophisticated, and much too revealing, electric blue dress. With her hair up and heavy makeup, she looked almost as old as her mother did. Of course, Charlotte looked very young for her age. Maybe Chelle hadn't been drinking. Gareth wondered if anyone would ask for her ID before she was served, since she looked more than old enough to drink. However, while it was ship's policy not to serve alcohol to minors, it was not strictly illegal when they were out to sea.

He pulled Doug back through the doorway, so they could converse and hear each other. "She's in there."

Doug frowned. "I didn't see any teens."

"She doesn't look like a teen." Gareth nodded his head toward the dance floor. "See the woman in the bright blue dress?" She had her head thrown back and was doing a twisting, shimmying dance—one that had the eyes of every man in the room glued to her. It left little to the imagination.

"That's Mrs. Halloran's daughter?" Doug's eyes almost popped out of his head. "I never would have recognized her from this picture. It's a good thing we were the ones to search up here."

Gareth had a sick feeling in the pit of his stomach. He didn't look forward to the rest of the evening. Charlotte would be upset and hurt, and he didn't want to be the bearer of the bad news, but it couldn't be helped.

"She might not come, or at least she may make a scene if I try to get her to come with me. You go in and get her to accompany you to my quarters, but don't tell her where you're taking her. Please be discreet, okay?"

Doug nodded, and Gareth hurried back down the stairs. He wanted to walk around the track and pray before he returned to his apartment. This could be a long, ugly night, and Charlotte needed all the divine intervention she could get.

Gareth punched the deck number on the elevator keypad and lifted the walkie-talkie from his waistband. He clicked the call button before speaking. "We found the lost item. Everyone return to your regular duties. Thank you for your assistance."

When he reentered his quarters, Charlotte glanced up expectantly. She looked past him into the empty corridor, and her face fell. "I had hoped they'd found her."

Gareth quickly crossed the room and pulled her to her feet. "We have. Doug is bringing her here." He nodded to Marilyn, and she left them alone, closing the door softly behind her. "I wanted to be with you when she arrived."

Charlotte pulled away and gripped her upper arms as if shielding her heart from harm. "Why? Has she been hurt?"

"No, she's just fine." Before he could continue, a knock sounded on the door. "Come in."

The portal opened, and Chelle stepped into the room. When she saw her mother, she crossed her arms over her chest where way too much skin was showing.

Charlotte gasped. "Chelle? Is that you?" She ended on a screech.

Gareth went over to thank Doug. When he did, he caught a whiff of alcohol on the girl's breath. Things were worse than he thought. Didn't the bartender ask to see her ID? He'd have to deal with that later.

After Gareth closed the door behind Doug, the silence turned as thick as molasses in January and throbbed with unspoken words. He looked at Charlotte, and his heart hurt at her stricken expression. He couldn't think of any way to soften the tension.

Charlotte crossed the room. "Where did you get that dress?" Her voice sounded hard and brittle.

Chelle stood straight and defiant, but she didn't answer.

"I asked you a question." Charlotte's voice rose as she stopped in front of her daughter. "Where did you get that dress? You didn't bring it with you like you did the bikini, did you?"

The teenager dropped her arms to her sides. "No. I bought it at the boutique with the gift certificate."

"You were planning this, weren't you? That's why you had your nails painted that color." Charlotte took the girl's hands and stared at them in disgust. "I can't believe you were so devious." She must have noticed the smell, because she wrinkled her nose and her face paled. "Chelle, have you been drinking?"

The question hung in the air for only a moment, before the teenager answered with a defiant shake of her head. "So what if I have?"

Charlotte pulled a hand back as if to strike the girl, then turned stricken eyes toward her own hand. She clutched her arms across her chest and strode across the room, stopping to stare out the windows into the darkness. No magic path of light here.

After a moment, she heaved her shoulders taking a deep breath and deliberately pivoted on one foot. "How could you drink that stuff? Have you forgotten that a drunk driver killed your father?"

Chelle looked as if her mother had slapped her, then red suffused her cheeks. Anger glittered from her eyes as she turned to glare at Gareth. He knew, at that moment, the girl hated him.

Without blinking, she whirled back toward Charlotte. "Why can't I forget? You seem to have forgotten all about Daddy."

Before Charlotte could answer that indictment, Chelle tore open the door and fled down the corridor.

nine

Charlotte followed Chelle at a distance and made sure she returned safely to their cabin. Then, not yet ready for another confrontation, she walked past the cabin door and out on a silent, empty deck. She gazed at the vast expanse spreading from horizon to horizon. "God, what am I going to do? Have I made a complete mess with Chelle? How can I reach her? How can I heal the breach that widens between us?"

She waited for an answer, hoping to hear an audible voice. None came, but peace stole into her heart. *A soft answer turns away wrath.* The words she heard so clearly in her mind came from the Bible, didn't they? Maybe she had just thought of them herself.

Don't try to deal with the problem until you are at peace yourself. Well, she sure wouldn't have come up with that. Had it been so long since she listened for God's voice that now she was having a hard time recognizing it?

"Lord, it'll be difficult not to continue what I started with her in Gareth's quarters. . . . I can't just let her get away with this, can I?"

Trust Me, Child. Give Me time to work on her heart. I'll let you know when to talk about it.

Charlotte knew that had to be the Lord. It went against everything within her. Maybe the Bible was right when it said that God's ways are higher than our ways and God's thoughts higher than our thoughts. She had to decide whether or not to trust Him in this. She knew she hadn't done such a good job on her own.

"Lord, it's not going to be easy, but I choose to do things your way." Talking aloud to Him out here under the vast canopy of midnight blue heavens studded with twinkling stars made Him feel closer than He had in a very long time. A new beginning. That's what she needed. A new beginning with the Lord. . .and in other areas of her life.

This thing, whatever it was, with Gareth would have to be put aside for now, maybe forever. Although Charlotte enjoyed the growing friendship, her daughter needed her, and that was what was most important.

When she finally got to the cabin, the lights were still on, but Chelle slept huddled in a fetal position under her sheet. Sprawled across her bed with her makeup smeared, curls rioting around her face, and clutching one of the pillows as if it were a shield, she looked so young. . .and hurt. Tatters of the blue dress were scattered around the floor. For a moment Charlotte was sorry Chelle had wasted her gift certificate by tearing up the dress. Of course the garment wasn't appropriate for her, but Charlotte had been so glad for her daughter to win something special. Hopefully she had some of her prize money left.

After undressing, Charlotte turned out the lights, but she left the drapes open, even though they would soon enter the Mississippi River. She wanted to look at the stars and keep the feeling of closeness to the Lord. When she finally fell asleep, her mind turned to fitful dreams. She awoke in only a few hours when the early morning sunlight poured through the bare window. She closed the drapes so it wouldn't also awaken Chelle.

Charlotte had forgotten to pack the suitcases last night and leave the luggage outside the door as the instructions said to do, so she and Chelle would have to carry theirs off the ship. She took a quick shower then pulled the bags from the closet.

꙰

Gareth spent most of the rest of the night praying for Charlotte and Chelle. He had no idea how their problems would be resolved, but he knew God did. By lifting them in prayer, he felt that he had a part in what God was going to do. Even when he went to the bridge before his ship entered the Mississippi, his prayers continued.

After they docked in New Orleans, his heart urged him to go see Charlotte and her daughter one more time before they left the ship, but he received a check in his spirit. Now wasn't the time. He would just have to trust God to take care of them. But he could go watch them disembark.

Before he stepped out onto the balcony, Doug hurried through the open door to the bridge. "The Hallorans didn't put their luggage outside their room. Do you think they forgot, or do they want to carry it themselves?"

Gareth thought for a moment. "I don't know."

"Would you like me to tell their steward to offer to help them?"

A good idea. "Do that."

Doug gave him an exaggerated mock salute, a joke they often shared. "Aye, aye, Captain."

Gareth chuckled as his friend walked down the hall whistling. What was that melody? A love song? Leave it to Doug to put his own spin on things.

When Gareth went out on the small balcony, crewmembers had just opened the hatch on the side of deck two. Gareth watched them as they scurried around completing each task assigned to them. They worked like a well-oiled machine. He had a good crew, well trained and loyal. He smiled at the brilliant blue sky with a few wispy clouds lazily drifting in a gentle breeze.

The cruise dock was a beehive of activity, and beyond that the city of New Orleans was just waking up. Since this area held most of the tourist attractions, activities flourished all night, so mornings were quiet.

When the first passengers disembarked, Gareth's attention turned toward the crowd pouring out of the ship's belly and crossing to the cruise building, where they would go through customs. With all the talking and laughter, they had obviously enjoyed the trip. That's what he wanted—for happy people to go home and tell their friends how much fun they had on the *Pearl of the Ocean*. Good PR. That's what Doug always said.

Finally, Charlotte and Chelle appeared on the gangplank. Although they each pulled a suitcase behind them, a room steward followed with two more. When they stepped onto the concrete dock, Charlotte turned to the man and tried to give him a tip. He smiled at her and refused. The travel agency she used had included a tip with the price of the cruise. Of course, it would have been appropriate if she gave him more, but the man must have understood that the captain wanted him to help the women. Gareth decided to give something extra to Doug for the steward.

Charlotte looked up just as she had before she boarded the ship. Her gaze connected with his and held for an indeterminate time. Her expression went from happiness to almost longing before she turned away and followed her daughter into the building. Gareth returned to the bridge. The connection between them was still there, but he knew Charlotte wouldn't pursue it. At least not right now. Maybe he shouldn't either. But, although his head made this rational decision, his heart couldn't agree.

❧

When Charlotte and Chelle deplaned at DFW Airport, their next-door neighbor waited by the luggage carousel. As usual, the baggage hadn't started coming from the airplane when Charlotte and Chelle got there. Charlotte went over and sat beside Linda in one of the chrome chairs with its leather sling back and seat. Chelle crossed her arms and walked restlessly around the room, milling through the crowd and glancing at every sign and poster, even stopping as if to read some of them. Evidently, she didn't want to be too close to her mother.

Linda turned to Charlotte. "So what gives? Didn't y'all have fun on the cruise?" Her worried expression followed Chelle's movements.

"Most of the time." Charlotte knew her voice sounded weary. That's what she was—weary of all the hassles. She took a deep breath and smiled at her friend. "There was a lot to do on the ship."

"The ship? What about the islands? Are they as beautiful as they look in the brochures?"

Charlotte felt thankful for the safe topic. "More beautiful than words can describe."

Linda frowned at her as if trying to read her expression. "Something bad happened, didn't it?"

They had been friends so long they could read each other's moods. "A couple of upsets with Chelle. The one last night was the worst."

"I'm sure you don't want to discuss things here." Linda patted Charlotte's arm. "Maybe after y'all are unpacked and Chelle has gone off to see her friends, you can come over for coffee and we can talk about it."

"If you'll make it a glass of iced tea instead, you're on."

When they arrived at home, Chelle went to her room and shut the door a little too hard. Charlotte gazed toward the ceiling, wanting to see through it right to the throne of God. *Lord, how long do I have to wait?*

Be patient. Good things always take time.

Charlotte wasn't surprised when Chelle soon came to the open doorway of her bedroom. "Mom, I need to go down to the store and check on my schedule. Mr. Stokes should have posted it today."

After waiting a moment to see if the Lord would give her any other direction, Charlotte nodded. "Sure, honey, go ahead."

A surprised expression flitted across Chelle's face. "I think I'll take the swimsuit back to Merry while I'm out, and if she wants to, we'll get lunch."

"All right." This patience thing wasn't easy. Charlotte wanted to forbid her to see Merry until this was settled, but she understood that wasn't what God would have her do. She would be reacting in anger.

A few minutes later, the phone rang. Charlotte glanced at caller ID. It was her neighbor, just as she figured. "Linda, I'll be right over."

"Good. I have some peach iced tea, and I made cookies before I went to the airport to pick you up."

"I'll come for the tea, but I'll pass on the cookies. You wouldn't believe the amount of food available on a cruise."

Even though it was only April, the Texas sun beat down on Charlotte's head as she crossed the yard. Maybe she should have a couple of trees planted in the front. The back was shaded comfortably, but not out here.

Linda met her at the door with the tall frosty glass. Charlotte took a long swig before she followed her friend into the den. She sank into the welcoming comfort of the smooth leather sectional sofa. Both she and Linda slipped off their shoes and pulled their feet up beside them, leaning against the deeply cushioned arms of the couch. Charlotte set her glass on the coaster waiting on top of the end table.

"Okay, I want to hear all about the trip, starting with the first day."

"Will Billy be home for lunch? It might take awhile."

Linda laughed. "It's Saturday. He's out on the golf course with some of his buddies. I don't expect to see him until the sun goes down."

Charlotte remembered the times Philip joined Billy on the golf course—not very often, but whenever he went, Philip always enjoyed it. In the past year, when she thought about something like this, it hurt so much she pushed the memory away. For some reason, today the thought didn't hurt as it used to.

"Have you ever been to New Orleans?"

"Never."

"Well, they bury people aboveground there. In little vaults that almost look like tiny houses." Even that thought didn't bring pain.

"What a gruesome thought." Linda took a drink of her own glass of tea then set it back down. "So what about the ship?"

"It was beautiful. Very elegant with lots of brass, plush carpet, glass walls and doors, even a large theater with entertainment from Vegas. One of my favorite places was the library."

"Wow. What else?"

Charlotte couldn't keep her mind off the tall, handsome captain. The expression in his blue eyes when he looked at her always warmed her heart. "The crew was topnotch, always trying to anticipate our every desire."

Linda studied her a moment. "There's something else, isn't there? A minute ago, you had a dreamy expression in your eyes. What gives?"

"Can't I keep anything from you?" Charlotte pushed her hair behind her shoulders. She should have put it up so she would have been cooler. But maybe it wasn't just the hair that made her feel too hot in the air-conditioned house.

Linda laughed. "You know better than that. So come on, girlfriend, spit it out."

What could Charlotte say about Gareth without her friend getting the wrong—or maybe the right—idea? "Well, the captain was single and very handsome."

"And?"

"And we got acquainted." There that should be enough without giving anything else away.

"Acquainted, huh? Just how acquainted did you get?" Linda's smile looked almost like a smirk, a knowing smirk.

"Okay." Charlotte took a deep breath. "If I had been interested in anything like that, we might have had a light shipboard romance."

Linda got that *I told you so* expression she often used. "That might have been good for you."

Charlotte held up her hand to stop her friend. "No way. When Philip died, the romantic part of me died with him. I'll never—"

"Just stop right there." Linda scooted closer to her, looking straight into her eyes. "You are a young, vibrant woman with a long life ahead of you. Never say never about anything. You don't know what'll happen, what God will bring into your life."

Never say never, huh? "It's only been a year since Philip died."

"Are you going to wear emotional widow's weeds the rest of your life? Do you really think that's what God wants for you?"

Charlotte got up and paced across the room to stare at the pictures spread along the mantel. Did God bring Gareth into her life? But what about Chelle? She pivoted. "The thing last night with Chelle had to do with Gareth being in my life. . . sort of."

Linda stood up and reached back for her glass of tea. "So Chelle didn't like the captain?"

"For most of the trip, she seemed to. I don't know why last night was different."

❧

Charlotte took a long time falling to sleep that night. Maybe she missed the slight movement of the ship, lulling her. When she finally succumbed to slumber, dreams flitted in and out of her mind. In every one of them, Gareth stood beside her. The fun they were having made her heart light and happy. When she awoke, she missed him a lot. The thought of never seeing him again felt like a sword piercing through her. She tried to shake off the feeling.

While she cooked breakfast for herself and Chelle, she wondered what Gareth liked for breakfast. They never shared that meal of the day. Maybe she should have felt guilty thinking about another man in the house Philip provided, but she didn't. For some reason, she felt that Philip and Gareth would have been good friends if they had ever met.

❧

By Wednesday, Gareth knew he was completely smitten with Charlotte. Every time he walked into a room, he almost expected her to be there. He missed her at his table in the evenings. Of course, he tried to be the perfect host, but he couldn't help wishing she were with him. She had eaten every dinner, except one, at his table. While he listened to the conversation going on around the group, his mind wandered to the other times when she had been there. Her dark curls, those clip things she used to scrunch her hair up on the back of her head, the filmy flower-print dresses she liked to wear.

"Captain?"

The questioning tone caught him unawares. He turned toward the dowager sitting on his left. "I'm sorry. I missed your comment, Mrs. Harrelson."

"I was asking whether you have been a cruise captain for very long, or did you sail on other ships?"

Gareth launched into an explanation, all the time telling himself that he needed to pay closer attention or these passengers might not recommend the ship to their friends. Dinner couldn't be over soon enough for him. Finally, everyone departed, and he headed to the bridge. With the restlessness he felt, maybe he could give Homer a long break.

Even on the bridge, he felt Charlotte's presence. He stepped out on the balcony and the memory of the soft perfume she wore the night they were out here made him long to have her back. Close enough for him to breathe in that fragrance. Close enough for him to touch. . .close enough for him to kiss.

ten

By the time the ship docked in New Orleans, Gareth knew he had to talk to Charlotte. He didn't have to be back on the bridge until after lunch, and he didn't want anyone intruding on his phone call.

Gareth went to the open door to the balcony. "I'm going ashore for a while. You'll be in charge."

Homer nodded and gave him a half wave. "I'll see you when you get back."

After exiting the ship, Gareth walked toward the taxicabs queued up in the street beyond the cruise dock buildings. He opened the door to the first one. "Take me somewhere quiet. I'll want you to wait for me while I make a private phone call. It might take awhile."

The cabby glanced back at him. "Sure thing." His thick southern accent resonated in the small confines of the automobile. From the wide, white smile that gleamed through his dark face, Gareth figured the driver envisioned his meter running up quite a tab.

The park where they stopped wasn't far from the dock area, but it met Gareth's requirements. Even though the day felt warm and muggy, a cool breeze blew through the trees and flowering bushes all around him. Gareth chose a wrought-iron bench sitting in the shade of a spreading magnolia tree. He enjoyed the scent of the waxy blossoms that were beginning to open.

Gareth punched the button that would ring Charlotte's

number. He'd programmed it into his cell phone soon after she left the ship. He had never been more thankful for the satellite instrument than he was at this moment. After several rings, he started to pull the phone away from his ear, but she picked up.

"Hello." Her answer sounded tentative.

"Charlotte?" Silence hung on the line between them.

"Gareth? Is this really you?" A breathless quality filled her voice, quickening his heart.

"Yes. . .I had to talk to you." He hadn't wanted to sound so desperate, but he did.

She laughed. "I almost didn't pick up the phone. The number showed as an unknown on caller ID, and I don't like to talk to telemarketers. Even though I signed up for the Do-Not-Call list, I still get some." She stopped as if she had run out of words. "Are you on the ship?"

The wind died down, but Gareth didn't mind the heat as long as he could talk to Charlotte. "No. We've docked in New Orleans. Actually, I'm in a park. I wanted complete privacy to make this call." Had he told her too much?

"I'm glad you called." Warmth infused every word.

Gareth took a deep breath and let it out slowly. "I've missed you. Everywhere I go on the ship, I remember seeing you there."

"Wow. I miss you, too. I enjoy my memories of the times we spent together, but since you have never been here, I don't have memories of you in this house."

He pictured her now with curls tumbling around her face and her eyes twinkling with an inner light. He had to think about something else. "How are things with Chelle?"

Charlotte seemed to hesitate. "Well, we still haven't dealt with it. I've prayed a lot, and I believe God is telling me to wait. That He will show me when to talk to her. He's working on her heart."

Gareth smiled even though she couldn't see it. "That sounds good. So have you moved closer to God? You told me you had blamed Him for letting Philip die."

"I finally realized that I need Him to help me with Chelle. We both have to work through this."

Gareth glanced at his watch. Their conversation felt so short, but he'd been here quite awhile. He really needed to get back to the ship. "I can call you when I get back into port, if you want me to." When she didn't immediately answer, he continued, "Or we could e-mail each other."

"Just call me the next time you're in port. I don't do a lot of e-mail."

"Okay. Will you be home next week at about this time?"

"Yes, and Gareth. . .thanks for calling today."

After they hung up, he ambled across the grass toward the taxi. He could call her from the ship, but he wanted to distance the relationship from his working day. How could he balance what he felt for Charlotte against his strong desire not to be hurt again. . .hurt as he was when he lost Britte? But he didn't want to face the thought of never having any contact with Charlotte again.

❧

If Charlotte thought about Gareth a lot the first week after the cruise, it didn't compare to the number of times he filled her mind the second week. She was so excited on Friday night that she had a hard time going to sleep. Before daybreak, her eyes popped open and she was instantly awake. This was ridiculous. She wasn't a teenager with a crush. On her next birthday, she would face the dreaded four-oh. So why did her stomach hold a flock of butterflies that could fill the Cotton Bowl?

"M–o–m?" Chelle came through the den with a huge towel wrapped around her body. Another one turbaned her hair. "Are you going to fix any breakfast today?"

Charlotte turned from the window where she had been watching a pair of cardinals peck the ground. "Sure. What do you want?"

Chelle reached into the cabinet for a small glass and poured herself orange juice. "You know, you haven't really cooked very much since we got home."

A feeling of guilt settled over Charlotte. Her daughter was right. "Maybe I was just spoiled by the way they waited on us hand and foot on the ship. I haven't given the house a good cleaning either." She leaned both arms on the tall bar between the kitchen and breakfast room. "You didn't tell me what you want to eat."

After downing the last of the juice, Chelle looked at her. "Anything. I'm just hungry."

"How about French toast?"

"Great." Chelle padded back across the den toward her bedroom.

Finally, the two of them felt sort of comfortable with each other again. Charlotte still heard the Lord tell her to wait. This was the kind of thing Philip would do. Ignore things and hope they would work out. She had always wanted to talk it to death, and usually that led to an argument. Maybe this way was better. But sometime, they would have to discuss what happened on the ship.

After Chelle ate and left for work, Charlotte looked at the clock above the end of the bar. What time did Gareth call last week? She didn't remember checking the exact time, but it was about midmorning. Just then, the phone rang. Her heart started beating double-time, making her feel breathless.

She glanced at caller ID, and her breathing returned to normal before she picked up the phone.

"Hi, Linda."

"What are you doing this morning?"

"Why?"

"I thought we could go down to Kohl's and check out the sale this weekend."

How could she get out of that? Linda knew how much she liked to shop. "I've let a few things go, and I really need to clean up this morning. Maybe I can get a rain check." That wasn't very convincing, was it?

"Are you okay, Charlotte? You sound a little. . .strange, I guess."

"No, I'm fine. I could go this afternoon. You don't think all the good things will be gone by then, do you?"

She finally got Linda off the phone. It couldn't have been more than a minute before it rang again with the same unknown phone number showing as last Saturday.

"Hello." Charlotte nervously tapped the fingernails of her other hand on the countertop.

"Is this a good time?" The vibrant baritone voice sent shivers through her. She was glad no one knew.

"Yes. Did you just get back?" Charlotte felt like she did when she was in high school, when she tried to talk to one of the football players, her thoughts all jumbled.

"Actually, we docked by seven this morning, but it took me awhile to get away. I want to be where no one could bother me. How are you doing, Charlotte?" The caring tone in his voice touched a spot that sprang to new life after more than a year.

"Things are on a more even keel here." She laughed. "I hadn't thought about it until now, but that's a nautical expression, isn't it?"

His hearty laugh reached through the phone line into her heart. "So it is. I'm glad things are better with you."

"How are Homer and Marilyn. . .and Doug?" Why couldn't she think of something more interesting to talk about?

"Homer is missing Marilyn; just like I'm mi— She went home last weekend. Doug's still here."

What had he started to say? Was he going to say he missed her, too? She hoped so.

The conversation lasted much longer than last week's, but he was drawing it to a close much too soon. "I'm going home to the Netherlands after next week's cruise. . .for my regular three months off. I'll call you when I get into port."

❧

The next Saturday morning, Charlotte woke just as early. Anticipation bubbled up inside her and simmered all morning. When the hands on the clock moved beyond ten, then eleven, she felt a letdown. Maybe he wasn't going to call.

Feeling more than ever like a teenager waiting on a boy to call, Charlotte decided she wasn't going to just sit around and mope. If he had tired of her, fine. Shopping would help her forget about him. . .if she could get her heart to cooperate. She didn't need these seesaw emotions at this time of life. She longed for that even keel she talked to Gareth about last Saturday.

Charlotte dug through the clothes in her closet and pulled out the new dress she bought last Saturday. She smiled as she remembered how good it looked on her. Linda wouldn't have let her put it back, even if she wanted to. But she didn't want to. The gauzy sundress had a draped neckline, and the exotic flowers reminded her of the butterfly garden she visited on the cruise.

After dressing, putting on makeup, and pulling her hair up

into a French twist, Charlotte slipped pearl stud earrings into her ears. Giving herself a once-over in the mirror, she smiled. She didn't look like a woman who was pining away over a man.

She walked into the den and picked up her purse, rummaging in it to find her car keys. The ringing of the phone distracted her, but she told herself not to get her hopes up. When she looked at the caller ID machine, Charlotte felt a reprieve.

"Hello, Gareth. I'd almost given up on you. I was just ready to leave the house."

"Where were you going?"

Did she want to tell him she was going shopping? "Just out."

A long pause echoed in her ear. "I don't want to keep you from anything important. . .but I'm at DFW Airport. I had hoped you could pick me up, and we could go out to eat before my flight to Oosterhout leaves later this afternoon."

The tom-tom beating in her chest sent a flush to her cheeks. Gareth was here at DFW. She never expected anything like this. "Okay. Tell me which terminal, and I'll be there in about fifteen minutes." Thankfully, she was already dressed.

❧

Gareth stood inside the terminal with his sports jacket over his arm and watched for the car Charlotte said she would be driving. When it slowed beside the curb, he quickly pulled his overnighter outside with him.

Charlotte got out of the car and opened the trunk. "I'm so glad you came."

After putting the luggage in the car and closing the trunk, he turned toward her. She looked so beautiful, and the warm wind blew her perfume straight toward him. He closed his eyes and inhaled quickly. After opening them again, he took her hands. "I am, too."

He couldn't keep from raising her fingers to his lips. So what if they were in public?

A blush stained her cheeks, and she sighed. "You clean up really nicely." Her nervous laugh revealed a lot to him.

"So do you." He slipped an arm around her waist and reached to open her door. "Where are we going for lunch? You're from here, so take me anywhere you want. Don't worry about the price. I want this to be special."

While she made a series of turns that took them out of the airport, he studied her. On the ship, he liked her hair down and even bunched up from the heat, but this style really flattered her. Curly tendrils kissed her cheeks and neck, giving him all kinds of ideas. *God, what am I going to do? She excites me as no woman has since Britte.* Too many obstacles stood in the way of a committed relationship, the only kind he would consider.

"Since you have such wonderful chefs feeding you all the time, it's hard to decide where to go." She smiled toward him before returning her attention to the road clogged with traffic.

At least on the ship, her attention hadn't been divided between him and all these vehicles. He almost wished he had her alone with him on the *Pearl of the Ocean*. "I just wanted to be with you, so whatever you want to eat is fine with me."

"How about lots of broiled meat? Isn't that what men like?"

He joined in her laughter. "Take me to it."

When they were seated at a table in a Brazilian restaurant, she leaned toward him. "I've always liked to come here, but I don't very often, because they just keep bringing the wonderful broiled meat by the table as long as you will eat it.

There's beef, lamb, chicken, pork, anything you want, and the salad bar is the best I know."

All through the meal, their conversation flowed comfortably. Gareth didn't want this time to end. The food was good, but the company was even better. Now he wished he had booked a later flight. Just thinking about being in Europe three months without the opportunity to see Charlotte made the future look bleak.

When the waiter took Gareth's credit card to run it through the machine, Gareth reached into the pocket of his jacket that hung on the back of his chair and pulled out a small, wrapped box. He placed it on the table between them.

Charlotte eyed the package almost as if it might bite her. "What's that?"

"A little gift for you." He pushed it closer to her.

"You didn't need to buy me a gift."

"I know." He smiled at her. "It's something I picked up on one of the islands. I meant to give it to you before you left the *Pearl of the Ocean*, but I didn't get around to it. It's sort of a souvenir of the time we spent together."

Charlotte carefully removed the bow and turned the box upside down. Without tearing it, she removed the paper and folded it on the table beside her. After lifting the lid off the box, she gasped and stared straight into his eyes. "They're lovely. You shouldn't have."

He leaned back in the chair and crossed his arms over his chest. "And why shouldn't I?"

"It's too much. A souvenir should be just a trinket."

"You looked at these a long time when we were in that store on Cozumel. I knew you liked them. Besides, a symbol of our time together should reflect the quality of that time. To me they were golden moments."

She relaxed, fingering the golden shells with pearls nestled inside them that formed the earrings. "They were for me, too. Thank you, Gareth."

❧

Chelle met her mother at the door. "Where were you?" She had beaten Charlotte home. "I called Mrs. Miller next door and asked her, but she didn't know."

Charlotte didn't want to upset Chelle. "I had lunch with another friend."

"You usually leave me a note telling me when to expect you. I was worried." Chelle went to the refrigerator and took out a can of soda, popping the top as she sat on one of the stools by the bar in the kitchen. "Where did you go? You're pretty dressed up."

Charlotte nonchalantly started pulling the pins out of her hair while she talked. "I had planned to go shopping, but then Gareth called. He was at DFW Airport on his way home to Holland for three months. He wanted to take me to lunch during his layover." She didn't look at Chelle, because she didn't want to see censure in her eyes. If she ignored it, maybe it wouldn't flare up.

"Oh." That one word held a world of meaning, none of which Charlotte wanted to hear. Chelle paused as if she wanted to say something else, then turned on her heel and stomped to her room, slamming the door behind her.

eleven

So much for an even keel. Once again, Charlotte stared at her daughter's firmly closed door and sighed. Now that school was out, Chelle went to work, to church, and out with friends, but when she came home, she barricaded herself inside her room with music so loud it blared through the walls. At least it was Christian music, but Charlotte couldn't really *get into,* as her daughter said, the raucous beat of some of the CDs. Before this standoff, they had shared a love of many of the contemporary Christian music groups. Charlotte kept KLTY playing on the radio when she was home. Now all Chelle listened to were the groups she knew her mother didn't like.

If only Charlotte could understand what the Lord was doing. She still felt the check in her spirit, keeping her from talking to Chelle about what happened on the ship that last night. They were at an uncomfortable impasse.

Charlotte looked forward to the phone calls from Gareth. Sometimes he stayed up late at night so he could call her in the evening. So far, the four or five conversations a week had been when Chelle wasn't home. Charlotte found herself yearning for those bright islands of peace, and something else she didn't want to define in their relationship, in her otherwise topsy-turvy world.

The youth group at church was meeting that night. Charlotte hoped something would happen there that could reach her daughter. She wasn't making any headway with

Chelle. She knocked on the closed bedroom door. When Chelle opened it, she was already dressed to go out.

"Did you want to eat before you leave?" Charlotte kept trying to make nonthreatening overtures.

Chelle shook her head. "No, I'm meeting a couple of the other girls at Bronco Bob's for burgers before group tonight."

Just as Chelle walked out the door, the phone rang. After reading caller ID, and despite her concern for her daughter, Charlotte smiled. She glanced at the clock and did a minor calculation before picking up the phone.

"Gareth, isn't it one in the morning there?"

"Yes. But I had to talk to you before I went to bed." She liked the sound of that. *He had to talk to her.*

❧

Gareth got a lot done during the three months he was home in the Netherlands. His sister helped him redecorate his house in Oosterhout. He hadn't changed anything after Britte died, and for some reason, he wanted to refresh and renew everything.

The best part of the time off from the ship was being able to call Charlotte often. Now that he was back in New Orleans and about to leave, that didn't have to change. Sitting on the big leather couch in the living room of his quarters on the ship, he punched in her numbers. He had told Homer not to disturb him for a while.

"Gareth."

He liked to hear her speak his name with that soft southern drawl, sounding like warm honey. "Charlotte, it was so good to see you again, even though I only had a short layover in Dallas. Your idea for a picnic was just right."

Charlotte laughed. "Eating it in the new international terminal, instead of outside, is a necessity in Texas summer heat. I don't do picnics during the hottest weather. At least not outside ones."

"I'm glad things have settled down some with Chelle." Gareth pictured Charlotte's laughing face he'd seen only yesterday. The hint of hurt had finally left her eyes.

"They have a new counselor in the youth group, who's connecting with Chelle. Last night she came home and asked if she could go on a special three-week mission trip with some of the youth. They're leaving Wednesday to go to Mexico and help build another building for an orphanage in Manzanillo."

Gareth stood up and walked to the windows. "That's a change for sure. Are you going to let her go?"

"I prayed a lot about it last night, and I believe God wants her to go." A sigh accompanied her words.

"But. . . ?"

"But it's a foreign country. . . . They'll be near the ocean where it might be dangerous. . . . And I'm afraid she might get hurt. Who will protect her? It's a long time."

Gareth imagined worry painting lines on her forehead. "If you've prayed, you have to trust her to God's care, don't you?"

❧

When Chelle came home from the final missions' team meeting, Charlotte sat in the den watching a classic movie. "Mom, can I talk to you?"

Charlotte hit the pause button on the DVD remote. "Sure. Let's get something to drink."

She went to the fridge for a couple of cans of soda then filled two glasses with ice cubes. "Do you want to sit here by the bar?"

Chelle's legs were longer, so she just dropped onto the tall seat. Charlotte had to hike herself up to reach hers, but soon they started sipping the colas. "So what did you want to talk about?"

"The cruise." Chelle put her glass down and stared at her hands cupped around it on the counter.

Now, Charlotte. The words sounded as clearly in her heart as if God were standing beside her speaking them into her ear.

"What about the cruise?"

Chelle glanced up at her mother. "Probably the last night, but really all of it. Why haven't you been on my case about it?"

Charlotte didn't expect that question. "I don't know if you'll understand this, but God told me not to say anything yet."

Chelle nodded. "I do understand. I've been fighting Him, but He's really done some things in my heart and life. Marsha— you know, that new counselor, Miss Connor—has been helping Him, I think."

"How?" This sounded promising to Charlotte. Maybe God knew what He was doing. *What am I thinking?* Of course God knew what He was doing.

"She's been helping me see what I was fighting against. And it wasn't you, even though it seemed that way. Does that make any sense?"

Charlotte stared into her own cola, watching the ice drift around in small circles. Had she been rotating her glass the way she often did? Evidently she had. Why did she always try to find something to take her own attention off of painful events? Maybe she and her daughter weren't so different. They both ran but in different ways.

"Yes."

"I wanted to slip out and see what went on late at night. I planned to dress so that I would fit in. Then I saw you in the library with the captain. You were sleeping, and he held you against his shoulder. It made me mad, so I planned to do something to hurt you. I didn't want you to look for another man to take my father's place."

Charlotte hoped the shock didn't show on her face. "I'm not looking for another man to take your father's place. Can't the captain and I be friends?" *If all I want is a friend, then why does Gareth feel like so much more?* Charlotte's gaze bore into her daughter's eyes, hoping to read her thoughts. "Besides, you do know you shouldn't have been in that club, dressed like that and drinking, don't you?" Charlotte tried to convey how she felt with a loving expression on her face.

"Yeah. It wasn't even fun. . . . And I didn't really enjoy wearing the bikini. I just did it as a form of rebellion. I understand that now." Tears streamed down Chelle's cheeks. "And I don't mind you and the captain being friends."

For a moment, Charlotte let that digest. She took a sip of her drink. "Miss Connor is good for you."

"Yes, she is. She's helping me get closer to the Lord." Chelle smiled through her tears. "Mom, can you forgive me?"

Charlotte pulled her daughter into her arms, and they both wept.

❧

Gareth paced through his office and out into the kitchen. He had told himself he would wait until he got back into port to call Charlotte, but he couldn't. He picked up his cell phone and punched the speed dial button.

"Hello, Gareth. Aren't you on the cruise?"

"Yes."

"I thought you weren't going to call me until you got back in port."

He had learned to tell how she felt by the tone of her voice. "But you're glad I did, aren't you?"

He heard Charlotte inhale deeply. "Do you know me that well?"

"I hope so." He tamped down his eagerness. "I missed

hearing your voice. We've talked so often the last three months. I couldn't wait that long."

"I know. It has been lonesome this week without your calls."

He thrust one hand through his hair that was getting a little long. "Did Chelle get off on her trip okay?"

"Yes. I had international service added to our cell phones. That way we can stay in touch if she wants to. I'm going to try and wait until she calls me."

He could hear the doubt in her voice. "Do you really think you can?"

"Maybe, maybe not. We'll just have to wait and see."

He leaned against the bookcase that sat under the windows across the front of his living room. "How about if you have something that will take your mind off her being gone?"

"I'm trying to stay busy. Yesterday Linda and I went shopping after the group left. And tomorrow, I'm going to help stuff the bulletins at the church office."

He laughed. "That's good, but I had something else in mind."

❧

Charlotte couldn't imagine what Gareth was talking about. "What's that?"

"How about coming on another cruise?" He sounded so eager.

"It's not in the budget right now. Although Philip had very good insurance, my money isn't unlimited. Our pastor is doing a series on managing our finances, and I'm trying to implement it." *What am I doing preaching to him?*

Gareth's rich laugh poured through the phone. "I meant as my guest. You know I can use a stateroom for guests without it costing me anything. It's a perk of the job."

A cruise sounded like fun, but could she do it? Or maybe the question should be was it a good idea for her to do it? "Why this sudden invitation?"

"The Voyageana Cruise Line is doing something different with the *Pearl of the Ocean*. This is the last trip from New Orleans. After the passengers depart tomorrow, we'll take the week to sail slowly to Galveston and prepare for our next itinerary. That will be our home port. I'd love to have you on the initial cruise from there. We'll leave on Sunday instead of Saturday, so the first departure will be a week and a half away. That should give you time to pack, and you'll be home before Chelle is."

How could she do it? Chelle might not like her being with Gareth that much, but she did say it was all right to be friends with him.

"We can even have your calls forwarded to my satellite cell phone, so you can receive her call when it comes."

When it comes. He sounded so sure it would. That encouraged Charlotte.

"And I'd be in a stateroom." She took a deep breath. "Which deck would I be on?"

"You could have the Penthouse Suite on deck eight. It has a baby grand piano. Or you can have an Executive Suite on the same deck. The other suites are booked."

"Why would I want a piano in my cabin?" She sounded eager even in her own ears.

"Some of the musicians can be persuaded to play for the people in that suite. It's rather nice."

Charlotte imagined the two of them sitting on a sofa, listening to live music in a fancy suite. Of course, she hadn't been inside one of those cabins, but when she booked the cruise she and Chelle took, she looked at pictures of the different cabins on the Internet.

"Are you sure it wouldn't cost you anything?"

"I wouldn't lie to you, Charlotte." His earnest tone touched her heart. "Even to get something I really want."

The last phrase sounded husky. Their relationship must be as important to Gareth as it was to her, which was almost a scary thought. "Okay. I'll do it, but I'm going to call Chelle tonight and tell her. If she doesn't like the idea, I won't come."

❧

When Charlotte's flight arrived in Houston, a limousine waited to whisk her to Galveston about fifty miles away. For some reason, although she knew there was a Galveston Island, she hadn't realized that the whole city was on the island. She had somehow pictured Galveston on the mainland with an island in the Gulf of Mexico near the town.

The car started up the incline of the causeway with water on both sides, and Charlotte felt as if they were driving in the middle of the ocean. She knew that was crazy, but she couldn't imagine traveling on the older causeway she saw over to their left, which sat so close to the level of the water.

The driver spoke into his radio and told someone that they were pulling up to the cruise dock.

"That isn't the ocean out there, is it?" She scooted closer to the front of the limo. "I see land on the other side"

The driver didn't take his eyes off the road. "The docks are on the Galveston Bay side of the island. Your ship will go around the east end to get to the Gulf of Mexico."

They passed two ships from other lines before they arrived at the Voyageana sign. Two crewmembers waited with a luggage cart. They loaded her bags onto it then escorted her through the crowd inside the building. At the VIP desk, Charlotte's key card was ready for her, and the young men guided her to a special gate at the front of the line. Everyone else waited behind another, larger gate.

"Isn't it too early to board the ship?" She tried to keep anyone else from hearing her question.

One of her escorts leaned toward her. "Yes, ma'am, but you're a special guest of the captain, so he told us where to take you."

Charlotte felt funny going ahead of all these other people, but she didn't want to cause a scene. She went through the area where the machine took her picture while her keycard was inserted. When they arrived where the ship's photographer took passengers' pictures in front of a large canvas poster of the ship, Gareth joined her. Instead of his uniform, he wore slacks and a sport shirt. That morning, Charlotte had a hard time deciding what to wear. She had always liked this pantsuit. It traveled well, but maybe she should have dressed up more.

"Thank you, men." Gareth shook hands with each of the crewmembers. "I'll take it from here." He turned to Charlotte with a smile. "You look lovely." His eyes traveled leisurely over her face. "After we have our picture taken, I'll take you to your stateroom."

Every time she saw him, her attraction to Gareth grew. Maybe this cruise wasn't such a good idea, especially since neither one of them was ready for a deeper relationship, but she would enjoy the trip. It would be something to remember if anything ever happened to end their friendship.

Gareth took her keycard from her and inserted it into the door. He followed her into the cabin. Charlotte looked at the opulence and could hardly believe this stateroom was for her. Not only was there a piano, the suite also contained a living room, a dining room with a refrigerator, and a separate bedroom with a king-sized bed. When she looked at the stateroom on the Internet, it said that bathroom even had a whirlpool tub. Each room in the suite had a wall of windows that opened onto a large balcony. Never in her wildest dreams would she have thought about occupying a suite like this.

Gareth stood and watched her as she discovered each part of the accommodations. "I'm glad you like it."

"I do." She slipped off her shoes and curled her toes into the plush carpeting.

Gareth took her hands in his, and tingles shot up her arm. "I'm going to put on my uniform and check the bridge. I'll be back for lunch."

"Aren't we going to the Oceanic Grille to eat like we did last time?" Charlotte had been so excited that she hadn't eaten much breakfast. She hoped to eat lunch soon.

"I've made arrangements for our meal to be served in here." He led her to the dining room area. "Your stewards only have this one stateroom to take care of. There are three of them to cover around the clock. Someone is available to bring you whatever you want twenty-four hours a day—food or anything else you need. That's one of the perks of the Penthouse Suite."

Gareth pulled her closer and gently kissed her temple. Charlotte held her breath, wondering if he would do anything else. Instead he moved back and let go of her hands. After pushing a curly tendril behind her ear, he walked to the door. Before he exited, he looked back at her, his gaze connecting with hers in a way that seemed almost a caress and continued for long moments. He finally closed the door behind him, and she took a deep breath. *What am I going to do about my erratic emotions?*

❧

After they sailed, Gareth took Charlotte to his quarters where Marilyn and Homer waited for them. Having the first mate's wife on the cruise gave Charlotte a welcoming feeling. Soon they were catching up over hors d'oeuvres and sparkling grape juice. Then the Wilsons went back to Homer's quarters, leaving both doors open.

Gareth led Charlotte into his office. She leaned against the doorpost and watched him open one of the drawers in his large desk. He pulled out a package wrapped in gleaming foil and sporting a huge lacy bow.

"Come here, Charlotte. I have a present for you."

Two pictures on his desk drew her attention. Eight by tens of the picture of Gareth and her at the captain's table and the formal portrait of her and Chelle were in separate carved cherrywood frames that matched his executive furniture. She picked up one of them.

"I didn't know you had these."

He moved so close behind her that she felt his heat through her summer clothes. "I've looked at them a hundred times since you were here. . . . Does it bother you that I have them?" His breath on the question disturbed her curls.

She had to think about that a minute. Did it? "Not really." She turned to face him, and they were almost touching. "I'm just surprised."

"Now"—he reached around her and picked up the box—"for your present."

Charlotte took the parcel when he offered it to her, but she wasn't sure what she felt about him giving her another gift. She reached up to her earlobe and felt the shape of one of the golden seashell earrings with the pearl in the middle.

"You've already given me a gift." She took a step back, but

the desk impeded her progress.

"It's just a token, a reminder of our times together." He leaned toward her. "Open it."

Her fingers felt like all thumbs as she tried to carefully remove the wrapping. He took the box from her trembling hands.

"Charlotte, you should just tear into a gift. Don't worry about saving the wrapping." He held the box in both hands while she followed his instructions.

Every time their skin touched while she tore at the ribbon and paper, a frisson of awareness sparked inside her. She felt as if she might go into meltdown if he didn't step back. Finally, she lifted the lid and gasped. Nestled in the snowy cotton, the amethyst necklace and earrings she had looked at on the last cruise sparkled up at her.

Her gaze shot to his. "Gareth, you shouldn't have—" His fingers stopped her sentence.

"Would it help if you knew that, as the captain, I get things at a very deep discount?"

She giggled, like a teenager, and then nodded. When his lips replaced his fingers, time stood still and her world tilted.

twelve

Gareth paced across the carpeted floor of his office and back to the doorway into his living room. When he couldn't sleep, he came in here thinking he would get some work done. That hadn't happened. He went through the door and dropped onto the couch, picking up the remote control and clicking on the TV. He ran through all the available channels, many more than the passengers had access to, but nothing caught his attention. With a disgusted huff, he turned off the glowing set.

His mind returned to the kiss. Although he and Charlotte enjoyed being together several other times during the day, all of them blurred into nothingness overshadowed by the moment their lips met. He had wondered if he really were falling in love with Charlotte. Now he knew. What had started as just a quick caress to stop her from questioning his gift quickly turned into more than he ever thought possible. Her willing participation in the kiss swept him along on waves of passion that threatened to drown him.

He hadn't wanted to put a name to that feeling before, but now he knew that he loved her completely. What was he going to do about it? What could he do? She had a home, a daughter, and a comfortable life in Texas. He lived in the Netherlands when he wasn't captaining his ship.

He rubbed the finger where he had worn his wedding ring, imagining another gold band encircling it. Even if they could decide where to live together, the kind of separation he and Britte experienced when he was at sea wasn't good for any couple. They lost touch with a lot in each other's everyday lives. He didn't want another relationship that evolved into what he had with Britte—secrets that caused tremendous pain when finally revealed. If, and it was a big *if*, he ever committed to marriage again, there would be no long separations. The *M*-word hadn't entered his thinking until now, but just the thought of what marriage to Charlotte would mean opened other doors in his heart. If they didn't accept their love for each other, they couldn't have any kind of relationship. After that kiss, he was sure she felt the same way he did. Did she think about never seeing him again? The thought of never seeing her again brought an ache that kept him awake and pacing the floor.

Gareth glanced at the clock. At 4:00 a.m. most of the passengers would be in their staterooms. What he needed was a good run to clear his head. He went into his bedroom and pulled on jogging shorts and a shirt. Soon he was the only person on the track that looped around deck ten, but physical exertion couldn't free his mind from the thoughts that had kept him awake.

❧

Charlotte turned over and punched at the pillow, trying to get into a more comfortable position. What was she thinking? This pillow welcomed her head with caressing softness. It wasn't the pillow that kept her awake. She shouldn't take out her frustration on it.

All through the rest of yesterday, she had forced the memory of that kiss to the back of her mind. The activity that accompanied the ship's departure from Galveston couldn't erase the effect the moment had on her. Gareth saved a place for her at his table. He later told her that he wanted her across the table, so he could look at her without excluding others.

Every time his gaze rested on her, she relived the feeling of his lips on hers, but she decided she wasn't going to bring it up to him. And he hadn't mentioned it.

When she arrived in this suite to go to bed, she couldn't keep her thoughts corralled. They were like the dolphins they saw around the ship, always jumping and diving, frolicking in the water. She had believed that the romantic part of her died with Philip, but she couldn't have been more wrong. The kiss awakened feelings she had almost forgotten and took them in an entirely new and different direction. Her response to the touch of his lips had been almost too much, as if her heart thirsted for it and finally she was drinking from the well. Before she could think, she put her whole heart and soul into returning the caress. What must Gareth think of her? Did her exuberant participation put him off?

Since he didn't mention it, maybe she had overwhelmed him, making him uncomfortable. Well, he had disturbed her comfort, too, turning everything she thought she felt all around into something she hadn't named before. If she didn't know better, she would think she loved Gareth. She had decided never to fall in love again. She didn't want to face the pain of losing someone, but breaking off contact with him would be like amputating an arm or a leg. . .or a piece of her heart.

Charlotte pulled back the drapes and opened the door to the balcony, going out to lean against the railing. Since the ship sailed at a good clip, a welcome ocean breeze blew her hair back from her face and cooled her cheeks. She wondered if Gareth was sleeping any better than she was.

❧

By Friday, Charlotte decided that Gareth wasn't ever going to mention the kiss. It didn't matter. The wonderful times they shared on the ship and the islands defined their relationship right now.

She brushed her curls up off of her neck and anchored them to the back of her head with a large claw clip. Although the temperature on the ship was comfortable, when she and Gareth got off at Cozumel, she would long for air-conditioning. A knock at the door of her suite brought her out of her musings. She quickly answered, knowing who stood on the other side.

"Charlotte, you look lovely today as always." Gareth raised her fingers to his lips. Above them, his gaze connected with hers. "Are you ready for our adventure today?"

As she nodded, she sensed a special excitement in him. What was he planning? He had said they would spend much of the day on the island, but although she enjoyed the excursions last time she was here, Charlotte didn't think any of them would bring this kind of feeling.

By the time they reached the open hatchway, most of the passengers who were going ashore had already exited. Gareth placed his hand at the small of her back and ushered her along the dock. They stopped so the photographer could take their picture behind the sign that proclaimed *Cozumel.* Soon they were in a taxicab. Thankfully, the air-conditioning was running as they drove away from the coastline.

"One of the older families on the island has recently turned the lower floor of their home into a restaurant and gift shop, no doubt needing to cash in on the tourist trade." Gareth leaned so close that his breath warmed her cheek. "One of the grandsons is on my senior staff. He told me to come to their place anytime, and I would get VIP treatment."

Charlotte laughed. "As the captain of a cruise ship, don't you always get VIP treatment?"

He threw back his head, and his hearty laugh filled the small confines of the compact car. "You are so good for me, dear Charlotte."

He clasped her hand and brought it to his lips, soundly kissing the back of it. Although there hadn't been a repeat of the heart-stopping kiss they shared on the first night, today he had already bestowed two kisses on her hand. Tropical vegetation lined the narrow paved road, with tree limbs intermingling above to form a corridor of shade. Various shades of bright flowers gleamed from within the lush greenery. Charlotte wished for one of the blossoms to stick in her hair. With her white peasant blouse and tropical print skirt, she would really look like an island girl.

"Here we are." Gareth opened the door and helped her out of the cab.

She studied the two-story house while he paid the cabby, telling him to return for them in two hours. The porch encircled the sides of the house that were visible to them. Charlotte assumed it went all around. An equally wide balcony spread above, with open doorways and windows allowing the breeze access to the upper floor.

A man with snow-white hair and brown, wrinkled skin met them at the door. "Señor Van den Hout, *mi casa es su casa.* Welcome." He ushered them to a private dining room.

After they were seated at the table beside a large open window, Charlotte looked around for a menu, which was nowhere in sight. A large ceiling fan above them sent a welcome breeze across their table.

Gareth smiled at the man. "Santiago, it's nice to enjoy your lovely home again."

"Are you ready for us to serve you?"

Gareth nodded and the man exited.

"So, what are we going to have?"

"All the specialties of the house." His noncommittal answer only raised more questions in her mind.

A young woman entered carrying a tray with small bowls of tropical fruit chunks, glasses of water, and cups of some kind of fruit punch. Charlotte frowned at the water.

"It's safe to drink. They use purified water here."

A procession of mouth-watering food followed, and Charlotte tried each item. Some she really enjoyed, but she only took a bite of the others. As usual, Gareth's knowledge of the history of the area made pleasant dinner conversation. When the dessert was served, she could only eat a couple of nibbles.

"Don't you like it? This is the best flan I've ever had." Gareth put another spoonful in his mouth, apparently savoring the burnt sugar flavor.

"Yes, it's good." Charlotte patted her stomach. "I've just eaten so much I can't hold another bite."

Gareth put his spoon down and pushed his dish away. He leaned forward and took her hand. "I asked for the private room, because we need to talk."

❧

Charlotte's eyes widened at his words. He had put this off until near the end of the cruise, because he didn't want her to think he was speaking just in the heat of the moment. They had spent a lot of time having fun together. Even Charlotte's conversations with Chelle had been pleasant. Now they needed to look at their relationship.

"I've come to care for you. . .a lot." He stopped and swallowed, then took another drink to wet his dry throat. He didn't know why this should be hard. He placed his hand on hers. "I love you, and I believe you return the feeling."

She turned her hand palm up and interlaced her fingers with his, grasping them tight. "I've had a hard time sleeping, because I was trying to understand what's happening between us. I never wanted to fall in love again."

"I know, Charlotte. I didn't either, but there's no denying the way I feel."

"What are we going to do about it?" Her voice sounded husky. Maybe her throat was as dry as his was. She took another drink of water.

"I'm not sure." He reached under their clasped hands and fingered her ring. "You're still wearing your wedding rings."

"I know. At first, I didn't want to take them off. Then I was afraid it would upset Chelle if I did."

He scooted his chair even closer to the corner of the table that separated them. "Do you want to take them off?"

"They're a symbol of the love Philip and I shared. That's important to me."

"We could have the diamonds reset into some kind of drop, maybe a gold nugget or something like that, and you can wear them to remember him. It wouldn't bother me." Gareth saw one of the girls peek in through the door, probably checking to see if they needed anything. He waved her off with his other hand. "I'll always remember my life with Britte. Anything you and I could have together would be different."

Charlotte nodded. "I know. It already is."

"But it wouldn't be any less real. I can't imagine living the rest of my life without you."

"Nor I you." Charlotte moved closer to him. "There are a lot of things standing between us."

"I know, but I want to share our lives." He stood and pulled her to her feet then led her to the window where they stopped and gazed into one another's eyes. He read the love coming from her heart. "I believe we can work out all the problems—time, place. . .anything."

Charlotte stood on her tiptoes and placed a soft kiss on his cheek. "I'm sure you're right, but I must think about Chelle. Nothing permanent can happen until she's comfortable with you in our lives."

Gareth wanted to pull her into his arms and replay the kiss they shared on the ship earlier in the week, but he knew it wouldn't be a good idea. Instead, he turned her face back up to his and restrained himself as he kissed her, not allowing it to turn into the passionate embrace they shared before.

Knowing that Santiago wouldn't give them a bill, Gareth pulled a couple of twenties from his billfold and placed them under his plate. "Let's go see what they have in the gift shop."

❧

Many of the shops on the islands were gaudy with merchandise crammed into a small space. When they had been on the island before, Charlotte hadn't wanted to shop there. But the brightly lit room they stepped into held tasteful displays of what looked like high-quality goods. They worked their way around the room, looking at a variety of items. Charlotte picked out a couple of T-shirts for Chelle. By the time they reached the back of the shop, she had added a purse for herself and one for her daughter, as well as a necklace made out of seashells for Chelle.

Gareth stopped beside a glass jewelry case. He picked up a brochure from a holder at one end. "This tells about the black coral found near the island." He opened the pamphlet and showed Charlotte. "The black coral beds in the Mediterranean Sea near Greece were harvested in ancient times until the corals died. They didn't realize the reef was home to living organisms." He pointed to one paragraph.

" 'For centuries, it was believed that there was no more black coral, until it was discovered in the waters of the Caribbean near Cozumel.' They monitor the harvesting of the black coral here to protect the reefs." He gave her the brochure to add to the ones they had collected earlier in the week.

Charlotte leaned over the glass and looked at all the items in the lighted case. She pointed to a gold chain with varying sizes of black coral, red coral, and gold beads. "That reminds me of the Add-a-Pearl necklace my grandmother bought me when I was a little girl. The pearls were graduated like this."

Gareth signaled the clerk to come over.

"What are you doing, Gareth?"

"Wouldn't you like to try the necklace on?"

Charlotte knew what he was doing. She was going to have to stop letting him know what she liked since he had bought the things she had liked the most.

"Charlotte, let me do this. It's been so long since I had a woman to buy things for. It gives me pleasure to make you happy."

When the woman took the necklace out of the case and placed it on top, she added drop earrings with beads to match. "These would look good with it."

"Yes, they would." Gareth undid the clasp on the chain and placed the cool metal and stones around Charlotte's neck. "It looks good on you."

The clerk held up a mirror, and Charlotte turned one direction, then the other to get the full effect. She liked the way the largest bead nestled at the base of her throat.

Gareth signaled the clerk to leave. "Since the black coral was believed to be lost, but then was found again, this can be a symbol of our love for each other. We have lost our first loves, but God is giving us a new love to replace it. You must let me buy them for you." He picked up the earrings and handed them to her.

Charlotte took off the colorful painted hoops she wore and slipped the golden posts into her ears. They did look good. She turned her gaze up toward his intense blue eyes. "Thank you." She wanted to kiss him, but with the woman hovering just out of earshot, watching their every move, she let her gaze express what she felt.

❧

After Charlotte arrived home in Bedford, she had two days to get unpacked and ready to pick up Chelle from the airport. The taste of Gareth's last kiss still lingered on her lips, reminding her of the new love that filled her heart. Every time Gareth had a break since she left, he called her. The phone conversations were wonderful, but Charlotte wished she were back on the *Pearl of the Ocean* with him. He had a little over two months until his next three months off. She could hardly wait for that time to come. Here she was an almost forty-year-old woman, and she felt like a teenager in love.

When Chelle's plane landed, Charlotte waited by the luggage carousel. The youth group streamed through the rotating door, and Chelle ran to hug her mother—a very different scenario from the last time they arrived at DFW Airport.

"Did you have a good time?" Charlotte patted Chelle's cheek. "I missed you."

"Mom, we talked on the phone at least every other day."

"I know, but I missed you anyway." Charlotte noticed that Chelle's arm was still around her back.

"A lot happened to me on the trip."

Charlotte looked for injuries, but saw none. She must have frowned.

"I'm not hurt, Mom." Chelle pulled away and turned in a complete circle. "See. What I'm talking about is inside me. God has really worked on my heart."

Chelle did look different. More mature somehow. Charlotte was glad she had agreed to this trip.

"So let's sit down, and you can tell me."

Chelle did drop into a chair beside her mother, but nervous energy kept her from sitting still. "I'm not sure I can talk about it right now. Maybe after we're home and things settle down." She stared at her mother. "I just wanted you to know that you'll see changes in me."

Charlotte relaxed against the back of the chair. "That's good."

Chelle hadn't stopped looking at her mother. "There's something different about you, too."

"I had a really good time on the cruise."

"I'm sure you did without a problem teenager to keep up with." Chelle laughed, taking the sting out of her comment.

"You weren't a problem."

"Of course I was." Chelle leaned back and looked to see if any luggage had come up to the carousel. "So what kind of room did you have?"

"You would have loved it. I was in what they call the Penthouse Suite."

&

In the week since Charlotte left the ship, Gareth called her every day. Finally, they were back in Galveston, so he could take all the time he wanted to talk to her. He first called her cell phone, but that went to voice mail. After leaving a message, he called the house phone.

"H—hello." A sob divided the word.

"Chelle, is that you?" Of course it was the teenager, but

something was wrong. "What's the matter?"

The girl's sobs had continued during his questions. "I—I just got home and found Mother—she's hurt! I don't know what to do!"

"Calm down, Chelle. Don't hang up!" He had to keep her on the line until he could find out what was wrong with Charlotte. Fear held his heart in a vicelike grip. "Now talk slowly and tell me what happened."

"She's on the floor." Chelle took a deep breath that ended in another sob. "She must have been cleaning the ceiling fan and fell off the step stool. I think she hit her head on the hearth. Her head's bleeding, and she's not awake."

Gareth wanted to jump through the phone and magically be there with them. "Have you moved her?"

"No, I was afraid to. I was looking for the phone to call 9-1-1 when it rang."

"Good girl." He let out the breath he had been holding. "Is your cell phone turned on?"

"Yes."

"Don't hang up this call, and use your cell phone to call 9-1-1."

thirteen

Gareth hadn't felt so helpless since he found out that Britte had advanced cancer. He couldn't dwell on that now. *God, please don't let Charlotte's injury be severe. I'm not sure I could take that so soon after our declaration of love.* At least Chelle had kept him on the line until the paramedics arrived. She even repeated what the men said to each other. The men hadn't liked the fact that Charlotte had not come to. He didn't either. Now they were on the way to the hospital. *Lord, please help me get to Charlotte somehow. I feel so helpless here. I know You're in control, and I believe You brought us together. Make it all work.*

Gareth couldn't stay here and wonder what was happening. He picked up his cell phone and punched in the number to the dispatching office at Voyageana. "Dirk, I have a problem. Is there anyone available to take over this cruise for me?"

"Let me check the computer." The familiar businesslike voice of the main dispatcher didn't sound as though it came from another country. "You're in luck. One of our substitutes lives in Houston, and he's not on another ship. I'll call him and get back to you. Is the problem something we can help you with?"

"I'm going to try to get a helicopter to take me to the Dallas-Fort Worth area as soon as possible. A very close friend was in an accident." Gareth felt his voice soften on the words *very close friend.* He hoped Dirk didn't notice.

"Hold off on that until I have an affirmative from the other captain."

The call abruptly disconnected, and Gareth stared at the display screen. He hoped he wouldn't have to wait long. Patience was a virtue, but not one he had mastered yet. He picked up the ship's internal phone and called the bridge.

"Homer, Charlotte has had an accident. I've called headquarters. They're trying to get you a substitute for this week."

"You can go ahead and leave if you want to." His first mate must have understood how upset Gareth was. "I'll wait for him to arrive."

Gareth rubbed the back of his neck and rotated his head. "Dirk said to wait to make arrangements until he gets back to me." Just then his cell phone rang. "I've got to go. That might be him."

"Van den Hout here."

"You're in luck, Gareth." Dirk's voice sounded more cheerful than last time. "Not only was Captain Hodges home, he has a friend who owns a helicopter. They'll fly down to Galveston, and the friend will take you to wherever you need to go."

The heavy weight on his heart lifted just a fraction. "Thank you." *How like You, God, to come through in a crisis with more than I ever imagined. That "thank you" was meant for You, too.*

Dirk gave him a few further instructions and hung up. Gareth had written down the name of the hospital where the ambulance took Charlotte. Harris H. E. B. He turned around to the computer and did a Web search of the name to get the phone number. The receptionist gave him all the information he needed. At least Chelle had the presence of mind to put his name down as a person who could receive information about her mother. What a relief that the hospital had a helipad and had assured him that he would be cleared to land when they arrived. After getting the coordinates to give to the pilot, Gareth quickly tossed some clothes into a bag. He wasn't sure how long he would be gone, so he threw in a few extras.

Everything happened quickly. In a little less than two hours, Gareth thanked the pilot and strode toward the front entrance of the hospital. Thankfully, the helipad was at ground level, instead of on the roof as with some hospitals. He knew August was the hottest month in Texas, but he hadn't ever experienced this kind of heat. On the coast, the ocean breezes lowered the temperature from the one hundred and six degrees he had noticed on a sign at a bank they flew over. He hadn't felt any air movement since he left the helicopter, and sweat beaded his forehead and ran down his back, plastering his shirt to him. When the double glass doors swooshed open, he welcomed the cool air.

"I need the room number for Charlotte Halloran."

The woman behind the tall wooden counter looked up from the papers spread out in front of her. "And what is your name, sir? I have to see if your name is on the list of people who can receive information about this patient." After he answered, she punched a few keys on the computer keyboard. "She's being taken care of right now, but her daughter's in the waiting room." She pointed to the hallway that stretched behind him. "It's the first door on the right past the elevators."

When he reached the walls of windows that lined the hallway on both sides, he saw Chelle. She sat with both elbows on the armrests of her chair and her head in her hands. He quickly crossed the room and dropped into the chair beside her. She lifted her head.

"Captain! What are you doing here? I thought your ship would leave today." She straightened and pushed her long hair behind her ears.

"It'll sail soon, but without me. I had to come see about Charlotte." He studied her expression, trying to gauge her reaction.

She gave a tremulous smile. "I'm glad you're here."

"Are you really?" The answer to that question might be a precursor for things to come.

She nodded without hesitation.

Not wanting to look as if he were overpowering her, he relaxed against the back of the chair. "Have you heard anything from the doctor yet?"

With a look of sadness and a little fear in her eyes, Chelle shook her head. "I keep hoping he'll come soon. There was so much blood on the floor."

Gareth had expected that someone would be with the girl, but no one sat nearby. "So did you call anyone to meet you here?"

"No. I wanted to wait until I knew how badly she was hurt." She heaved a huge sigh.

"Chelle, you shouldn't have been waiting alone. Isn't your neighbor a very good friend?"

A doctor stepped through the doorway, and Chelle watched him expectantly until he called out another name. "She wasn't home, so I just came by myself."

Gareth wanted to pull the girl into his arms and comfort her, but he didn't know how she would react. He already loved her like the daughter he never had, since he and Charlotte had discussed her several times since the cruise.

"Did you call the church? Surely someone from there could have been here with you."

Tears pooled in big blue eyes, so like her mother's. "I didn't even think about it."

"I will be here as long as I'm needed."

Chelle turned a weak, watery smile toward him. "Thank you, Captain. I don't know why, since I was such a problem on your boat."

Gareth laid his arm across the back of her chair without touching her. "Let's forget about that, shall we? You and your mother have worked it all out, haven't you?" One of these days he'd explain to her the difference between a boat and a ship, but now was not the time.

She nodded. "But I'm ashamed of what I did."

"Remember, we're going to forget about it. I will if you will." He opened his eyes wide, cocked his head, and looked straight at her. "Do you think you could call me Gareth instead of Captain?" He liked this newer, softer Chelle.

"Is anyone from the Halloran family here?" The masculine voice intruded into their conversation.

They had been so engrossed that they hadn't noticed the man enter the room. Both of them jumped up and hurried toward him.

"Mr. Halloran?"

Gareth almost laughed, but he wasn't sure Chelle would appreciate it. "No, I'm just a good friend, but this is her daughter."

Chelle stepped between him and the man in the green scrubs. "How is my mother?"

"I'm Dr. Bruton. I was on duty when your mother was brought in." He crossed his arms over his chest and smiled at Chelle. "Mrs. Halloran isn't hurt as badly as it looked from all the blood. Even superficial head wounds bleed a lot. She has a cut on her scalp. I had to shave a small space around the wound so I could put in the stitches, but at least the scar will be covered with her hair. She did sustain a concussion from the blow, so I want to keep her here overnight. Sometimes head wounds are tricky. I just want to be on the safe side, and the insurance company agreed."

Gareth was glad the doctor took the time to explain so much to Chelle. She needed it. He had watched her, and some of the tension in her shoulders slowly relaxed while the doctor talked to her and the deep grooves between her eyebrows softened.

"When can I see her?" Chelle's voice didn't sound as wobbly as before.

"We'll have her in a room pretty soon. The nurse will come give you the number when we know for sure what it is. She can take you to the room to wait." He held out his hand to the teenager. "Let me know if you need anything else from me."

After shaking his hand, Chelle watched the man exit then turned to look up at Gareth. "He was nice, wasn't he?"

"Yes." Gareth put his hand behind her back to steer her to the chairs they had occupied before. "Could I get you something to eat or drink?"

She fingered the hem of her T-shirt. "I'm not hungry."

"Have you had anything to eat today?" Gareth thought she looked pale and wan.

"I spent the night with a girlfriend, and her mom fixed us a big breakfast before I went home. It wasn't so long ago, because we stayed up almost all night talking, so we slept pretty late." Chelle studied his face for a long moment. "Do you need something? It's after noon now."

"I can wait." He wasn't going to leave the girl alone again, and he'd had a good breakfast, too, even though it was very early that morning.

A nurse came through the doorway. "Halloran family?"

Chelle jumped up and raised her hand above her shoulder. "Right here."

The nurse continued toward them. "Your mother's room is 304. Would you like to go up there now?"

Chelle nodded and the woman led the way.

After the nurse left them at the room, Gareth offered Chelle the most comfortable chair and took the straight one. "I guess all we can do now is wait." He leaned forward and propped his forearms on his thighs.

"Capt—um, Gareth, or should I call you Mr. Van den Hout?" Chelle grinned at him.

"No. Gareth is fine. I hope we can be friends."

"You told the doctor that you were. I assumed you meant Mother's friend. Do you want to be mine, too?"

Well, she didn't mince words, did she? "I'd like that."

She stood up and went to the window to open the blinds. "No wonder Mother likes you so much." She turned around and leaned against the windowsill.

"Do you mind?" Gareth hadn't been ready for this conversation, but maybe now was as good a time as any.

"I did at first, and you know it."

Silhouetted against the slats of bright sunlight streaming through the window, her expression was hidden from him. Gareth cleared his throat. "But I told you I choose to forget, remember?" Was this a test?

"Yes, you did. That just shows how nice you really are. And I like the changes I see in Mother. She acted like an old woman this past year, and I know why. I felt some of that, too. I miss Daddy. I'll never stop missing him."

Gareth stood up and put his hands in the pockets of his slacks. "You shouldn't. . .but it will grow less painful over time."

A nurse stuck her head in the doorway. "Mrs. Halloran will be here in about fifteen minutes."

"Thank you." Gareth and Chelle answered in unison; then they smiled at each other.

When the door closed behind the nurse, Chelle stood up straight. "Has Mother told you what happened to me in Mexico?"

"Yes." He rubbed a finger across his forehead. "You do know we talk on the phone almost every day."

Chelle nodded.

"What do you think about that?"

"Gareth, what are your intentions toward my mother? I don't want her to be hurt." Chelle sounded stern.

Once again, the teenager surprised Gareth. "What if I told you I want to marry her?"

"Do you?"

"Would it be all right with you if I did?"

"I know there would be lots of things you have to work out for it to happen, but if you can do that, then I'm for it." She turned earnest eyes toward him. "Does that surprise you?"

"Yes, I thought it would take longer to convince you." Gareth smiled.

"A man who would drop his job, a very important job, and come to see about my mother must love her very much." Chelle held up one finger, then a second. "A man who cares about her teenage daughter, even though she has been bratty around him, is a good man." A third finger went up. "Mother told me that you are a Christian, and not just in name only. Those are three things in your favor. You aren't going to want her or me to forget my father, are you?"

"Of course not!" Gareth's exclamation bounced off the walls of the small room, so he modulated his tone. "And I won't forget my first wife either. The love I feel for your mother is different, but equally as strong, and because of her,

I love you, too, Chelle."

Tears glistened on her eyelashes, and she moved closer to him and slipped her arms around his waist. He hugged her back. "I won't take your father's place, Chelle. I want my own place in your life."

When Chelle pulled back, he reached for the box of tissues and handed her one. Another minute like the last one, and he'd need a tissue, too. He leaned his head back and squinted his eyes, trying to contain the tears that threatened to fall.

❧

When Charlotte opened her eyes in the hospital room, Chelle stood at her bedside. "Mom, you're finally awake."

"How long have I been out?" Her head itched, but when she reached to scratch it, her hand encountered a bandage. "And what's this?"

"I'm afraid you're going to have a terrible headache when your medication wears off."

She would know that voice anywhere, but she hadn't expected to hear it here in Bedford. She could remember snatches of things—being on the stepladder, the wail of a siren, pain while the doctor examined her, then nothing until now. When had Gareth come into the picture?

"Mom, Gareth got a substitute and had a helicopter bring him to the hospital. He waited with me." Chelle was smiling, so she didn't seem to be upset about it.

Charlotte looked beyond her daughter to the tall man standing behind her. "Hi. I'm glad you came." She turned her attention back toward Chelle. "Didn't you call Linda or someone else to wait with you?"

"I wanted to see how bad you were hurt first."

"How did Gareth find out?" His blue eyes studied her just as intently as she was studying him. He must have run his fingers through his hair because it looked rumpled, like a boy who didn't like to use a comb or brush, but nothing else about him looked like a boy. He was all man—tall, strong, and handsome—as he stared back at her with a loving expression in his eyes.

"He called right after I found you." Chelle smiled at him over her shoulder. "He stayed on the line while I called 9-1-1 on my cell."

"Chelle told me everything the paramedics said. . . . I just couldn't stay on the ship and worry about you. I had to come see for myself."

Charlotte started to turn her head, but a hot blade of pain made her stop.

"Do you need some more medication?" Gareth moved toward the door. "I'll get a nurse for you."

"We can ring for one right here." She held up the cord with the button on the end.

"Of course you can." He moved closer to the bed, shaking his head as he came. "I don't know what I was thinking."

Charlotte pushed the button and told the nurse what she needed. "Who's running the ship, Homer?"

"No." Gareth leaned toward her and took her hand. Chelle pushed the straight chair over for him to sit on. "He'll soon be a captain, but not yet. We do have substitutes when we need one. Captain Hodges lives in Houston. He came right away, and his friend brought me up here in his helicopter."

She could hardly believe how much trouble he went to. And Chelle didn't seem to resent his presence. Even though Chelle had changed a lot since the mission trip, Charlotte had wondered how she would react when she found out about what had happened with Gareth. "It helps to have friends in high places. Will you rejoin the cruise during the trip?"

"No, I'm staying here until you're better. Captain Hodges told me to take as long as I needed." He squeezed her hand. "I have to make sure you're completely okay before I go."

Chelle cleared her throat. "I think I'll go get something to drink. Gareth, do you want something?"

The look that passed between the man she loved and her daughter caused a catch in Charlotte's throat and warmed her heart.

"I'd like a tall glass of iced tea." Gareth laughed and pulled a bill from his wallet. "I can see why all you Texans drink yours iced instead of hot. The heat here is ferocious."

Chelle snagged the money and giggled as she went out the door, almost colliding with the nurse bringing Charlotte's medicine.

"This might make you sleepy." After injecting the pain medicine through her IV, the nurse picked up Charlotte's arm and counted her pulse. "I'll have to check on you often."

The woman left, and Gareth pulled the chair back beside the bed. Before he sat down, he leaned over and placed a soft kiss on her forehead.

"I think you overshot, didn't you?"

Gareth laughed. "I didn't want to hurt you."

"I believe a kiss is just what the doctor ordered."

When he complied, she almost forgot the pain that pounded in her head.

❧

Charlotte enjoyed having Gareth close by. He'd rented a room at a hotel on Airport Freeway, but he hadn't used it much, since he spent so much of his time with her and Chelle. After chauffeuring her to have the stitches out this morning, he told her he wanted to take her out for dinner tonight and she should dress up for it. Then he left, telling her he wouldn't be back until time to pick her up for dinner. It was the first day this week he was gone so long.

Charlotte had finally convinced Chelle to go to work as scheduled. They really needed her on a Saturday. With no one else at home, Charlotte called the beauty salon and was able to get a last-minute appointment for a manicure. She also wanted to ask her beautician's opinion on how to clean her hair without disturbing the wound.

After she arrived at home, she went into the bedroom and studied the upswept style. Jennifer had used some substance that cleaned the hair without hurting her scalp. When she found out Charlotte had a date with an important man tonight, she insisted on putting Charlotte's hair up before doing the spa manicure. The nail polish she used was a brighter color than Charlotte usually wore, but Jennifer talked her into it.

I don't look bad for an older woman. Charlotte giggled at her thought. What was she going to wear? He said dress up, but how much? Everything in her closet looked old to her. She hadn't bought anything new—except a few things before the first cruise and that one sundress—since Philip died, so she went to the back of the closet and looked through the things she had stored there. One of the dresses she'd always loved caught her eye. It had always made her feel feminine. The timeless chiffon with a full, sweeping skirt and draped neckline fit at the waist, emphasizing it. Impressionistic flowers splashed across the white background in varying shades of pinks, lavenders, and reds. One of them was the exact shade as the nail polish. She brought the dress out and hung it on the closet door. What should she wear with it? The amethyst jewelry Gareth gave her would look wonderful.

Excitement roiled inside her as she slipped into the

fragrantly scented bubbles in the bathtub. A leisurely bath felt decadent in her usually harried schedule.

I wonder where we're going. I might be dressing up too much. Somehow, she didn't care.

❧

When Gareth rang the doorbell, Charlotte answered the door. A swirl of soft fabric clouded around her, setting off her spectacular coloring. He wanted to sweep her into his arms and kiss her senseless.

"You look ravishing, Charlotte." He cleared his throat, hoping to get the huskiness out of his voice. It wouldn't do for her to guess what he had in mind. If he was too emotional, she might.

She peered past his shoulders and her eyes widened. "Is that a limousine?" Her gaze darted to collide with his.

He smiled. "I can't very well pay attention to you if I'm trying to follow directions to the restaurant, can I?"

She reached up and pressed a kiss to his cheek, then took a tissue from her tiny gold purse and wiped the lipstick off his face.

"Don't you want anyone to see it?" He laughed.

A blush crept up her cheeks. "I don't want you to be embarrassed."

"Then you had better bring your lipstick and more of those tissues with you." He raised his eyebrows suggestively before he crooked his elbow toward her.

She pulled the door closed behind her, and they went to the waiting car. The driver stood beside the open back door of the gleaming white sedan.

As they headed toward Dallas, Gareth was glad he wasn't driving. The freeways were busy, and he'd meant what he said to Charlotte. He pulled her closer under his arm and, with the fingers of his other hand traced the shape of her chin before turning her face up toward his. After his lips descended to hers, he savored every nuance of the kiss. Not as passionate as the first one on the ship, it packed a powerful punch of its own. He thought maybe they shouldn't indulge in too many of these yet.

When their lips parted, she pulled out another white paper square and dabbed it over his mouth. Then she reapplied her lipstick. Maybe she felt the same way he did since she wasn't waiting to do the repairs. He would honor her implied wishes. The night was still young.

Charlotte looked out at the buildings they were passing. He did, too. Many of the windows were lighted, and the structures were silhouetted against the twilit sky. He usually didn't like spending time in large cities, but everything looked beautiful to him tonight. Not all the rosy glow came from the setting sun.

The driver really knew what he was doing. He carefully made his way through the traffic to their exit near downtown Dallas.

"Where are we going, Gareth?"

"If I'm right, we're almost there." He evaded her question.

The driver stopped at the base of Reunion Tower adjacent to the Hyatt Regency Hotel. He got out of the car and opened the back door. Gareth emerged and offered his hand to Charlotte.

"Are we eating here at the hotel?" Charlotte's gaze swept the glass doors and shiny accents as she alighted from the vehicle. "I've never been inside."

Gareth nodded to the driver. He'd made his arrangements before they arrived at Charlotte's house. The man would park the limo close by and wait in the hotel restaurant for a call from Gareth.

"We can go in there if you want to, Charlotte, but I made reservations at Antares."

She gaze followed the length of the tower to the giant lighted ball at the top. "Up there?"

"If that's okay with you." He whispered against her hair, stopping long enough to inhale the soft scent, somehow different today, but nevertheless intoxicating.

She clapped her hands like an excited child. "I've always wanted to go there, but I never have."

Chelle was right. Her parents hadn't ever been there together. *Good.* The teenager hadn't been completely sure when she suggested the restaurant.

They were seated at a table by the windows as he requested. They watched the skyline of Dallas creep by while they ordered and ate a delicious gourmet meal. The pace of the revolving floor was so slow that patrons didn't really feel the motion, but the view gradually changed. Brightly lit, Dallas at night spread like a multicolored tapestry before them. As soon as they finished their cherries jubilee, the waiter removed the dishes and disappeared into the shadows. When Gareth made the reservation, he had requested privacy. He was glad the waiter complied.

Gareth picked up the crystal goblet of sparkling grape juice and tipped it slightly toward Charlotte. "A toast to our love."

When she gently tapped her glass against his, a musical ping sounded between them. "To our love." She took a sip and set the glass down.

He slipped his hand into the pocket of the suit he bought yesterday. Earlier in the week, Chelle had shown him where they sold tall men's clothes. First he took out the letter she wrote to her mother.

"Charlotte, will you marry me?"

Her eyes sparkled in the candlelight. "I know Chelle accepts you into our lives, but I'd have to ask her before I can give you an answer."

He placed the letter on the table between them. "I knew you'd say that. She wrote this to you."

Charlotte picked it up and opened the envelope, scanning the message quickly before she looked up. "She knows you're doing this tonight?"

"She helped me plan it." Gareth chuckled. "That girl has a lot of ideas."

"Yes, she does, and she's a real romantic." Charlotte's eyes twinkled. "Since we have Chelle's blessing, I happily accept."

"Do you want me to get down on one knee to ask you again?" He felt a wrinkle between his eyes. How he hoped Chelle was wrong on this one.

Charlotte glanced at the other diners spread across the dimly lit room then smiled at him. "Was that Chelle's idea, or yours?"

"Hers, but I'm willing." He took Charlotte's hand and lifted it to his lips.

"Sitting here near me is just fine. I don't want to make a spectacle of ourselves." She whispered conspiratorially.

Gareth reached into the other pocket and brought out a tiny velvet box. He opened it to make sure everything was all right. He wasn't sure why he did that. The ring was in it when he placed it in his pocket. Why wouldn't it be there now?

"Do you want me to put this on your finger?"

"I'd like that." She lifted her left hand toward him. Love glowed in Charlotte's eyes, warming his heart and making him want to loosen his tie and let some cool air in.

When the ring slid on, Gareth thanked Chelle silently.

Every detail, except that kneeling one, was perfect. Soon they would be in the limo, and he would seal this commitment with an unforgettable kiss, more powerful than their first one had been.

epilogue

Two Months Later

For the third time this year, Charlotte Halloran flew into Houston to go on a cruise. But this trip was something she never would have imagined in her wildest dreams. Her wedding would take place on the voyage, and an excited, fun-loving entourage of friends and family deplaned with her.

After making their way through the sprawling airport to the luggage claim area, they spread out around the lane designated for their flight number. The happy chatter going on around Charlotte made her feel loved and at peace. Chelle gave her mother a hug, then hurried over to talk to her cousin. Charlotte could hardly believe that Gareth had made arrangements for over fifty people from Texas to go on the cruise and attend the wedding. Even Charlotte's pastor would perform the ceremony. His wife was almost as elated as Charlotte to be on this trip. Hank and Margie said they would consider it a second honeymoon.

Before he left Bedford the weekend he asked her to marry him, Gareth made arrangements with Pastor Hank to do his premarital counseling on several phone calls using the speakerphone in Pastor's office. Charlotte enjoyed taking part in the long conversations. The two men quickly became good friends, which didn't surprise Charlotte, since she loved both of them.

The first of the luggage bounced down from the conveyor

belt. She would have to pay attention, because she didn't want to miss hers the first time they came around and have to wait for them to make the long trip back.

"Charlotte."

When she heard Gareth's voice, she whirled toward the sound. He stood so close she was surprised she hadn't felt him arrive. His arms slid around her and pulled her close. Without a moment's hesitation, she threw her arms around his neck and leaned into his embrace. A sparkle in his eyes accompanied the questioning hesitation. She pulled his head down and kissed him. She didn't care that they were in the middle of a busy airport with lots of people to witness their love. The last two months apart had been hard. Although she talked to him, usually more than once a day, she missed his touch.

When their lips parted, someone clapped. Others joined, and Charlotte heard someone speak above the noise, telling the crowd that they were here for the wedding. Her cheeks burned, and she hid them against his broad chest.

"Did you miss me as much as I missed you?" Gareth whispered against her hair.

She nodded, not moving her head from where it rested. Soon everyone's attention reverted back to retrieving his or her luggage.

"I have a whole fleet of vans waiting outside to take everyone to the ship." His eyes seemed to devour her face, like a starved man looking at a long, overflowing banquet table. He brought one hand up to cup her cheek. "I don't want us to ever be apart this long again."

A lump formed in Charlotte's throat. "Me neither."

❧

When the vehicles pulled up to the Voyageana building on

the cruise dock, the crewmembers Gareth had handpicked waited to take the wedding guests' luggage aboard the ship. As when Charlotte came on the cruise in early August, the entire group with her went straight to the VIP desk where their keycards were waiting for them.

Gareth had made sure the staterooms he had chosen for them on deck eight were cleaned early this morning, so he could take them there immediately. Charlotte, Chelle, and their neighbor, Linda Miller, were in the Penthouse Suite— the same one Charlotte had before. Until the wedding, Linda's husband and Gareth would share the suite across the hall. It was smaller than the one where the women were, but larger than most of the others, with two separate sleeping areas. After the wedding, Chelle and Linda would switch rooms with Gareth.

Since it was too early in November for holiday travelers, he had been able to get the larger staterooms for everyone else, although they were scattered up and down that deck.

When everyone had their keycards, they all went through the check-in point where their security pictures were taken. A ship's photographer waited for them in the Centrum. So did a small group of other tourists.

"Charlotte, these are a few of my cousins from the Netherlands." Gareth's heart swelled with pride as he watched them welcome his bride.

After the introductions, the photographer's assistant clustered the whole crowd on the large, spreading staircase that led from the Centrum lobby on deck four up to deck five's elevators. When she was finished, the photographer stood by the balcony railing on deck six and took several shots from different angles before the Texas crowd had family boarding pictures made.

Gareth walked up the staircase to deck six and caught everyone's attention. "You have a couple of hours to settle in. Then come to the Dancing Waves Ballroom at the rear of this deck." He gestured that direction. "Our lunch will be served there."

≈

Charlotte and Gareth quickly ate their food, and he went to the bandstand and stood by the microphone. Charlotte thought he had a commanding presence even in civilian clothes instead of his uniform. Her pulse kicked up a couple notches, making her feel breathless.

"I'll just give you a quick rundown of the schedule while you continue eating. Then you can ask any questions you might have. We'll try to answer them." He held out his hand toward her and when she joined him he put an arm around her waist. "We'll be at sea two days, moving toward Jamaica. Tomorrow you can get acquainted with the ship in between preparing for the wedding. The rehearsal is on Tuesday morning in the Footlight Theater on deck five, and the wedding will take place there at 4:00 p.m. There is additional balcony seating for the theater on deck six. However, I assume most of you will want to be down close. Some of the crew will come to the ceremony, and we will let as many of the passengers come as space will allow, so you might want to get there early. After the wedding, we will have a reception for just our invited guests in the Monterrey Bay area next to the conference rooms right outside that doorway." He pointed toward the area. "After the reception, Charlotte and I will spend the night in the Penthouse Suite, and Chelle will spend the rest of the week with the Millers in their stateroom. Do I need to warn you that anyone who disturbs us will be thrown overboard?"

Laughter and hoots erupted across the room.

"Besides, there will be strong guards outside our door."

Charlotte felt a blush make its way up her cheeks.

"Does anyone have any questions?" Gareth asked.

Hands went up all over the room.

He laughed. "Let's take them one at a time, shall we?" He pointed to one of the Dutch cousins.

"Where are you going to live after you are married?"

Charlotte had expected that one to come up.

"We will keep both our home in Texas and our home in Oosterhout."

Charlotte laid her hand on his arm and moved toward the microphone. "It'll be nice to have the house in Europe as well as in the US. I hope to spend time in Holland soon, and I'm sure Chelle will want to tour the continent at some point. Maybe she can go over there for the summer when she graduates." She smiled at her daughter.

Chelle jumped up, and her fist shot into the air. "All right!"

"For now"—Gareth placed his hand on the middle of Charlotte's back—"we'll spend a lot of time in Texas."

"When you're not at sea."

Charlotte couldn't tell who said that, but she felt Gareth stiffen slightly. "Actually, I'm not going to continue captaining a cruise ship on a regular basis. Voyageana Cruise Line is opening a cruise-only travel agency in the Dallas-Ft. Worth metroplex. I will be the supervisor for that facility. I'll also serve as a substitute captain for the line. Hopefully, I won't be needed in that capacity very often until after Chelle graduates from high school and goes to college. Then when I do go on a cruise, Charlotte can be with me."

Charlotte tried to remember what other hands had been raised. She thought Billy Miller had been one of them. "Billy, did you have a question?"

All eyes turned to her neighbor, who liked to kid around a lot.

"So whose idea was it for all of us to come along on your honeymoon? Did you think we needed to protect you, or does Gareth need us?"

Charlotte was waiting for the laughing and cheers to die down, trying to think how to answer him, when Gareth leaned toward the microphone.

"Actually, I have a surprise for my bride." He glanced down and gave her a wink. "We are spending our wedding night on the ship, but when we arrive at Jamaica, a helicopter will take us away to a private Caribbean island that belongs to the president of Voyageana Cruise Line. We will spend the next week and a half in his villa there."

Charlotte's eyes widened, and she gasped. While everyone cheered, she turned toward him and pulled on his hand until he lowered his head near hers. "It sounds wonderful, but I can't leave Chelle alone that long."

He chuckled and put his arm around her. "She won't be alone. The Millers and the Larsons will take care of everything." When he gently kissed her temple, her heart melted.

&

While the ship's orchestra played a romantic medley, Gareth peeked out at the auditorium from behind the opened curtain on the stage. The place was packed.

All the seats near the front were filled with family and friends. Behind them an irregular section of white uniforms told him that many of the crew were here. Even though an announcement had been made over the PA system throughout the ship, he hadn't expected so many passengers to attend. Maybe most of them were romantics, or at least the women were. Probably they had to drag the men with them.

He smiled at that thought. A few months ago, he wouldn't have believed that he would get married again. How wrong he had been. He looked forward to every single day with Charlotte.

The music changed signaling the time for him, Homer, and Doug to move out and take their place beside the pastor in front of the orchestra. Gareth quickly looked toward the back where Linda Miller started down the aisle, walking in cadence. When she reached halfway, Chelle followed her. After they both climbed the steps up to the stage level, the music changed to "The Wedding March."

Charlotte stepped into the aisle, and he couldn't keep the tears from forming in his eyes. With flowers twined in her hair and a filmy veil fluttering down her back, she looked like an angel. The off-white gown she wore glowed like a precious pearl. She was precious to him. He couldn't take his eyes off her. Billy Miller walked beside her. Because of the slope of the aisle, she had to watch where she stepped, but she soon turned her eyes toward him and smiled.

❧

When Charlotte looked up toward Gareth, she almost lost her footing, but Billy steadied her. Who could have guessed that she would find another love in her lifetime? She remembered telling Linda several months ago that it would never happen. Maybe *never* should be banished from her vocabulary.

A Letter To Our Readers

Dear Reader:

In order that we might better contribute to your reading enjoyment, we would appreciate your taking a few minutes to respond to the following questions. We welcome your comments and read each form and letter we receive. When completed, please return to the following:

Fiction Editor
Heartsong Presents
PO Box 719
Uhrichsville, Ohio 44683

1. Did you enjoy reading *Never Say Never* by Lena Nelson Dooley?
   ❏ Very much! I would like to see more books by this author!
   ❏ Moderately. I would have enjoyed it more if

   _____

   _____

   _____

2. Are you a member of **Heartsong Presents**? ❏ Yes ❏ No
   If no, where did you purchase this book? _____

   _____

3. How would you rate, on a scale from 1 (poor) to 5 (superior), the cover design? _____

4. On a scale from 1 (poor) to 10 (superior), please rate the following elements.

   ____ Heroine   ____ Plot
   ____ Hero   ____ Inspirational theme
   ____ Setting   ____ Secondary characters

5. These characters were special because? _____

_____

_____

6. How has this book inspired your life? _____

_____

_____

7. What settings would you like to see covered in future
   Heartsong Presents books? _____

_____

_____

8. What are some inspirational themes you would like to see
   treated in future books? _____

_____

_____

9. Would you be interested in reading other **Heartsong
   Presents** titles? ❑ Yes ❑ No

10. Please check your age range:
    ❑ Under 18   ❑ 18-24
    ❑ 25-34   ❑ 35-45
    ❑ 46-55   ❑ Over 55

Name _____

Occupation _____

Address _____

City, State, Zip _____

Hearts♥ng

Presents

Great Inspirational Romance at a Great Price!

Heartsong Presents books are inspirational romances in contemporary and historical settings, designed to give you an enjoyable, spirit-lifting reading experience. You can choose wonderfully written titles from some of today's best authors like Andrea Boeshaar, Wanda E. Brunstetter, Yvonne Lehman, Joyce Livingston, and many others.

When ordering quantities less than twelve, above titles are $2.97 each.
Not all titles may be available at time of order.

SEND TO: **Heartsong Presents** Readers' Service
　　　　　　　 P.O. Box 721, Uhrichsville, Ohio 44683

Please send me the items checked above. I am enclosing $ _____
(please add $2.00 to cover postage per order. OH add 7% tax. NJ
add 6%). Send check or money order, no cash or C.O.D.s, please.

To place a credit card order, call 1-740-922-7280.

NAME _____

ADDRESS _____

CITY/STATE _____ ZIP_____

HP 8-06

HEARTSONG PRESENTS

If you love Christian romance…

$10.^{99}$

You'll love Heartsong Presents' inspiring and faith-filled romances by today's very best Christian authors…DiAnn Mills, Wanda E. Brunstetter, and Yvonne Lehman, to mention a few!

When you join Heartsong Presents, you'll enjoy four brand-new, mass market, 176-page books—two contemporary and two historical—that will build you up in your faith when you discover God's role in every relationship you read about!

Imagine…four new romances every four weeks—with men and women like you who long to meet the one God has chosen as the love of their lives…all for the low price of $10.99 postpaid.

To join, simply visit www.heartsong presents.com or complete the coupon below and mail it to the address provided.

Mass Market 176 Pages

- -

YES! Sign me up for Hearts♥ng!

NEW MEMBERSHIPS WILL BE SHIPPED IMMEDIATELY!
Send no money now. We'll bill you only $10.99 postpaid with your first shipment of four books. Or for faster action, call 1-740-922-7280.

NAME_____

ADDRESS_____

CITY_____ STATE _____ ZIP _____

MAIL TO: HEARTSONG PRESENTS, P.O. Box 721, Uhrichsville, Ohio 44683
or sign up at WWW.HEARTSONGPRESENTS.COM